Free of a
Dream

Free of a Dream

by
ADEL PRYOR

ZONDERVAN PUBLISHING HOUSE
GRAND RAPIDS, MICHIGAN

Free of a
Dream

CHAPTER ONE

A chilly autumn breeze rustled in the oak trees, scattering tawny leaves over the hospital grounds. But the sun shone brightly, and lawns and gaily-colored flower beds basked in its glory and warmth.

Inside the office it was cool, almost cold. That was the one thing Penelope Fielding had against the office — it faced south. Rarely did the sun reach the windows. Sometimes in midsummer, very early in the morning, the sun would venture into the room, but by nine o'clock, the time Penny usually arrived at the hospital office, the sun was fast disappearing from the window.

But the medical superintendent preferred it that way. He seemed to dislike anything that was warm and gay. He liked the cool air, the fresh breezes. Everything about him was cool and controlled and somber. Very seldom did he display any warmth of feeling, much to the young girl's secret sorrow.

Her reverie was interrupted as the door opened. Penny turned from the window.

"Good morning, Matron," she greeted dutifully.

"Hullo, Penny! Hope you enjoyed the long weekend," Ruth van Rhyn spoke pleasantly.

The young girl pulled a wry face. "Not much."

"Thought you were going away for Easter."

"I was. But then changed my mind. I'm sorry now."

The weather had been perfect, ideal for bathing and boating. It had been almost like summer, not a cloud in the pure blue South African sky, the sun hot and baking. But Penny had stayed at home waiting for Michael to call, which he had done so frequently in the past when her father was alive. Now she had waited in vain. Michael had neither phoned nor called. Only Don Anderson had come and Penny was getting tired of his

7

attentions. She had no intentions whatsoever of marrying that young Ear, Nose and Throat consultant, no matter how determined or persuasive he was. For her there would never be anyone but Michael — Dr. Michael Ashmore, Medical Superintendent of Oakhurst Hospital.

Penny debated for a moment whether to confide in Ruth van Rhyn. But she couldn't expect Matron to understand. Matron was getting on towards middle age — well, not exactly, but nearly. She must be about thirty-five. Of course, Michael was older. He was thirty-eight. But then, it was different with a man. An older man was so much more exciting, Penny decided, especially someone as distinguished looking, as handsome and elegant as the medical superintendent. Beside him other men faded into insignificance.

"I see you have already arranged flowers in Dr. Ashmore's vase." Ruth sounded slightly disappointed. She was holding a bunch of white carnations in her hand. "I managed to persuade James to let me have these to put on Doctor's desk."

Penny smiled. "Then you must have done some persuading." There was a mocking edge to her sweet voice. She knew as well as did the rest of the hospital staff the gardener's aversion to having to cut his precious blooms.

"There's another vase somewhere." Penny went to the cupboard.

"Never mind, my dear. I'll put them on my desk instead."

"They're beautiful," the young girl observed, looking at the blooms. *Fit for a bride,* she thought. Her blue eyes held a dreamy expression.

Tentatively Ruth began: "Did you manage to attend church at all on Easter Sunday?"

Penny's dreamy expression vanished. She wished fervently that Matron would leave off the subject of church attendance. Penny just wasn't interested. Because once as a young teen-ager she had accompanied Ruth van Rhyn to church, it didn't give her the privilege to —

Matron's voice intruded. "We had a lovely sunrise service on Easter morning. Fortunately I was free to attend. That reminds me — I shall be off duty this coming Sunday evening. Perhaps you'd care to come along with me?"

"No, thanks." The girl shook her chestnut colored head. Then she saw the disappointed look in Ruth's fine eyes. Penny said swiftly: "I did enjoy that Sunday school anniversary service you

8

took me to when I was about fourteen. That must be five years ago now."

Ruth nodded. She had been close to the young girl in those days. She had been the confidante the motherless Penny so badly needed. On her way home from school, the girl would generally call in at the hospital to see her father, who before his death had been an eminent neurosurgeon. Ruth held the late Henry Fielding in high esteem. She took an immediate liking to his pretty, petite daughter with her pert little nose and contemplative blue eyes filled with secret dreams.

Ruth, who was then assistant matron, had been delighted when the great Mr. Fielding had allowed his daughter to accompany her to the service.

"I shall permit you this special privilege of taking my daughter to church. You know I don't hold with church going. But Penny seems to have taken a fancy to you. It will do the child good, no doubt. Only don't ever ask me to come as well," he had added with one of his rare smiles.

It grieved Ruth that such a brilliant man should have lived and died without God.

The events of that Sunday were still vivid in Penny's memory. How thrilled she had been to accompany Miss van Rhyn to the anniversary service. Her father, though kind and generous, had been an austere man, lacking in understanding for his only child. He had given her everything except the kind of love and sympathy an imaginative, impressionable child like his daughter needed.

She had returned from church, her face still aglow with the wonder of it all. It was the first time in her short life that she had ever attended a children's service. How she had enjoyed the singing! And the beautiful illustrated talk about the Prodigal Son that the pastor had given had stirred her youthful imagination.

Miss van Rhyn had stayed to Sunday dinner, but had left shortly afterwards as she was back on duty at the hospital in the afternoon. Michael Ashmore had also been present.

Michael! Again Penny saw his face, his pale, clear-cut features and slightly sardonic mouth. He had teased her unmercifully that afternoon.

She heard again his voice. "Dear little Penny. You are so sweet. Please remain as you are. As a saint you'd terrify me.

9

Our Miss van Rhyn is a fine woman — a goodlooker, too. But, quite frankly, her religious zeal makes me shudder."

Michael was an agnostic. No, not an atheist. He would not dare to presume there was no God.

He and Penny had had a lively discussion. Finally the girl had bowed to the doctor's superior knowledge and he had since remained in her dreams as her ideal man. Dr. Ashmore didn't go to church, so why should she, Penny had asked herself so many times.

That was five years ago. Since that day her relationship with Matron had not been the same. Michael Ashmore had become her new confidant and Ruth had watched with some concern their growing friendship. She continued to pray daily for the girl.

Now, as secretary to the medical superintendent, Penny was more than ever under Dr. Ashmore's influence. There was no need for the girl to work. Her father had been a wealthy man. But she had insisted upon earning her own living. Ruth could admire her for that. Penny was a quick, neat worker.

"Penny — " Smiling, Ruth extended a hand. "Won't you please think it over?"

The girl furrowed her brow. "Think over what? Oh, you mean about coming to church with you. I've already said no!"

"It's because of Dr. Ashmore, isn't it?" Ruth ventured.

The color mounted the girl's cheeks. "I'd rather not discuss it, if you don't mind." She observed the hurt in Matron's eyes. "Well, if you must know, it's just that Doctor has no time for church going. You know that for yourself, Ruth. So why ask me?"

"I wanted to be sure, that's all. But please, Penny, don't let yourself be guided too much by what Dr. Ashmore believes or says. You yourself are accountable to God."

"Michael is a fine man," Penny countered, rising gamely to his defense. "Even you will have to admit that."

Unconsciously, Ruth's lips formed into a tender smile.

She nodded. "I agree. Michael Ashmore is a splendid man. But he has no time for God. That makes me sad. It would be wonderful if he belonged to the Lord. And you, too, Penny."

The girl made no comment. Then she said: "I'm glad you like Michael. I think he's terrific. I wonder why he has never married?"

Ruth hesitated before replying. "No doubt he has been too

10

engrossed in his work to bother with women. The hospital comes first with him."

"Hm . . . . Perhaps you're right. But I know he admires a pretty woman." Penny paused. "Ruth, do you think I'm pretty?" There was an anxious note in her voice.

The Matron smiled, considering the other's clear complexion, dreamy blue eyes, soft chestnut hair and sweet lips.

"Of course you are! As a young girl you were merely pretty. But now you possess a loveliness that is more than just surface prettiness. Don't let the world and all it seems to offer you ever spoil you, Penny."

"You do sound serious. Why, Doctor!"

The door had silently opened. Michael Ashmore advanced into his office. He greeted Ruth courteously, but his eyes were on Penny.

Ruth picked up the carnations.

"Don't go, Matron. I'd like to discuss the Radford boy with you." Dr. Ashmore turned to Penny. Her eyes were alight with admiration.

"Well, how are you? Had a pleasant weekend? My house-keeper gave me your message to say you'd changed your mind about going away. Sorry I wasn't able to phone you back."

Penny felt herself flush. She was conscious of Matron's eyes upon her. Much to the girl's embarrassment, Michael went on: "No doubt you had young Anderson to keep you company."

Penny dismissed the E.N.T. consultant with a shrug. Holding back her chagrin, she walked into the adjoining room which she used as an office.

Without speaking, the doctor followed Penny. He took off his jacket and expertly shrugged his lean shoulders into a white surgical coat. Then he stepped back into his office where Matron was still waiting for him.

As usual, Michael had dropped his jacket onto a chair. Penny placed the jacket on its hanger behind the door. She stood for a long moment fingering the fine material.

Then, with a sigh, she leaned her head against the jacket. Presently two bright tears rolled down her cheeks and came to rest on the sleeve of the coat.

CHAPTER TWO

In vain Penny tried to concentrate on the medical reports she was typing. Through the slightly open door she could hear Doctor and Matron discussing the Radford boy. Penny could have closed the door, but she didn't want to shut out the sound of Michael's voice. She loved listening to his smooth, deep tones.

"The whole affair is very tragic," Ruth van Rhyn was saying in her calm, clear voice. "But Dr. Anderson did a fine piece of surgery on the boy's ear. There is every possibility that Robin's hearing will not be impaired."

"Yes, so I believe." Dr. Ashmore stretched his long legs and pursed his lips thoughtfully.

Against her will Ruth found her thoughts straying. She was very conscious of the man's hard, lean form. She liked his long straight nose with its sensitive nostrils, and the way his blond hair was brushed back from his temples. His mouth, though sardonic at times, was usually set in pensive lines. But she had certain reservations about his steel-gray eyes. They were not happy eyes. They were coldly, tantalizingly aloof.

As if aware of her regard, the doctor considered the woman sitting opposite him. He had known Ruth van Rhyn for as long as he had been at Oakhurst Hospital. He was doing his internship; she had just been appointed staff nurse. He had heard that she was religious, and so he had avoided her whenever possible. He realized now that he scarcely knew anything about Ruth van Rhyn as a woman. He had not been interested enough to study her. However, he was fully aware that she was a competent matron, firm and fair-minded, and the nursing staff held her in high esteem. That was all that mattered in Michael's eyes. Her private life was no concern of his.

Now, irrelevantly, he wondered why she had not married. She

was good-looking enough, attractive in a quiet way. She had expressive eyes, an intelligent forehead and gently smiling lips. Her calm, cheerful presence had consoled many a fearful and distressed heart. She was really a credit to her profession, and, Michael mused, to the God in whom she expressed such faith and trust.

Suddenly Dr. Ashmore smiled. It was so unexpected that Ruth was momentarily at a loss for words.

"I was just thinking . . . we've known each other for almost fourteen years. Don't you think it's high time you and I called each other by our first names? In private, that is."

Ruth returned his smile. "A good idea. I've been wanting to, Michael," she confessed without embarrassment.

"Good! Now we can proceed. I'd like you to give me all the details of the Radford case. No, not medically. I've all that in this report in front of me. Tell me something about his family background."

Penny, trying to be busy in the adjoining office, thought, *Matron and Doctor seem to be on very cordial terms. But Michael can't really like her, that is, not in any special way. Ruth is too staid, well, for someone as smart and sophisticated as Michael.*

Doctor was asking Matron: "Do you believe the boy actually intended to shoot his stepmother?"

Ruth shook her dark brown head. "No — not for a moment. The whole thing was a ghastly accident. He merely meant to frighten his stepmother by pointing the pistol at her. Robin was certainly in a rebellious state of mind, but he had no intention whatsoever of firing. He tripped and fell, and the pistol went off accidentally. The bullet hit his ear, as you know. It's a mercy he wasn't killed."

"H'm . . . ." The doctor stroked his chin reflectively.

The matron went on: "I wouldn't take any notice of those reports in the paper, Michael. Some news reporters like to hint at a situation that just doesn't exist. Their insinuations can be pretty embarrassing to the parties concerned. The boy's parents are both suffering deeply. Robin's stepmother loves him as if he were her own son. Now, if Robin Radford had been the son of an ordinary man, I doubt whether the news would have reached the papers." Ruth spoke with deep feeling.

"You sound as if you know the Radford's personally. Am I correct?"

"Yes. Leonora is a friend of mine. We were at school together.

You know, of course, that Leonora Radford is Clyde Maxwell's sister?"

Michael's pale brows raised slightly. "Our house doctor? You don't say! But that young intern is as poor as the proverbial church mouse."

Ruth smiled. "He may be materially. But in a spiritual sense he is rich beyond compare. Clyde is a splendid Christian—"

Dr. Ashmore held up a deprecating hand. "Please, Ruth—"

She smiled apologetically and continued: "To return to Robin. His late mother spoiled him dreadfully. Poor woman! She had no option, it seems. She was weak physically. She simply could not stand up to her demanding son. She gave way to every wish and whim of his. Mr. Radford wanted to send Robin to boarding school, but his wife wouldn't even consider the idea. I don't blame her in the least, though. Robin was her only child. Her husband was often away, being a member of Parliament."

"But she could have accompanied her husband. Their son would have been well taken care of at boarding school. I see from the papers that Robin blames his father for his mother's death. Mr. Radford was away at the time when his wife had her fatal heart attack. The boy has frequently been heard to say that if his father had been at home his mother wouldn't have died."

"What nonsense! Mrs. Radford was a sick woman. Her husband was absolutely devoted to her. Mr. Radford waited three years before remarrying. He fondly thought that Robin had got over his mother's death. But how wrong he was! The boy would not forgive his father for marrying again. He resented his step-mother's presence from the moment she put her foot in the house. What a situation for Leonora. Yet not once have I heard her complain."

The medical superintendent rose. He had rather enjoyed his discussion with Matron. She could be a stimulating companion, he realized. Suddenly he felt a strange desire to know her better.

He found himself asking: "Doing anything special this evening? I'm free myself. Perhaps you'd care to eat with me?"

Ruth was conscious of the hot color stealing into her cheeks. But with perfect composure she responded, "I have a church meeting tonight. But thanks all the same, Michael."

"Perhaps some other time then." He motioned her to precede him out of the office. Together they walked down the hospital

14

corridor, he feeling oddly disappointed, she checking the pleasure his presence invariably evoked — in fact, had evoked for fourteen long years.

Penny, from her office, heard the door close behind them. She thought in disgust: Fancy Ruth turning down Michael for a church meeting!

She went into the medical superintendent's office, saw the carnations matron had left behind on the little table, picked up the blooms and walked purposefully in the direction of Robin Radford's room.

A serious-looking young man with spectacles was coming out of the room. Penny recognized him as Clyde Maxwell, the house doctor. Previously she had not taken any particular notice of him, but now that she knew he was the brother of the new Mrs. Radford, Penny eyed him with some interest.

He was tall, though not as tall as Dr. Ashmore. The intern's shoulders were sturdy, his mouth strong, yet sensitive. His hair was light brown and slightly wavy.

He looks like a fine person, she mused, *Good and kind. But not weak.* There was about him an air of strength that was not too obvious at first sight.

His greeting, though amicable, held a hint of deep respect. Penny was touched. Apparently to Clyde Maxwell she was not the child Michael Ashmore seemed occasionally to consider her.

Impulsively she extended her free hand. His clasp was cool and firm.

"I'm sorry, Dr. Maxwell — truly I am. Poor misguided boy! And your sister. How is she taking it?"

A gentle smile softened the serious face. Penny noticed that the eyes behind the spectacles were warm and sympathetic.

"Very well, thank you. I was staying with Leonora at her husband's home in Constantia when the accident occurred. I was not on call on Easter Sunday or yesterday."

"So you actually witnessed the accident?"

The intern shook his head. "Yesterday afternoon I was sitting in the garden trying to read. Robin's voice kept on intruding. He's a high-spirited youngster and inclined to be difficult to control. Through the open French windows I could hear him arguing with Leonora. The boy wanted to go swimming at Hout Bay. But as he had just recently recovered from flu, my sister thought the water would be too cold for him. She knew that her husband, had he been at home, would not have approved.

So she suggested to Robin that he swim in the pool at home. But the boy was determined to go. He threatened to run away and drown himself. He was shouting himself hoarse and was coughing badly. I was almost tempted to intervene, but somehow I managed to restrain myself and to stay where I was."

Clyde paused. His face was very grave.

Penny smiled sympathetically. "Please go on, Dr. Maxwell."

"Suddenly all was quiet. I thought Robin had yielded at last. But not so. Instead, he must have gone to take the pistol from the cupboard which as a rule was kept locked. The maid admitted she had forgotten to lock it."

"Oh." Penny's face registered horror.

The intern went on: "I don't for a moment believe Robin intended to shoot — he just wanted to frighten my sister. Next instant I heard a shot. Well — you know the rest, Miss Fielding."

"I'm sorry," Penny reiterated, feeling the inadequacy of words. "Where is your sister staying now?"

"At home with her husband. Mr. Radford flew back as soon as news of the accident reached him."

Penny was silent. Clyde Maxwell smiled uncertainly. "I must be getting back to Casualty. Thank you for your interest, Miss Fielding."

She smiled back. *He is nice,* she thought.

Penny ventured into Robin's room. The boy was lying quite still, the right side of his head swathed in bandages. Near the bed Matron and Dr. Ashmore were in deep consultation with the E.N.T. consultant. Their voices were scarcely audible.

Don Anderson was the first to become aware of Penny. He left off speaking to smile a greeting. Then he resumed his conversation.

Penny's sympathetic heart was touched as she studied the hapless boy. *He must be about twelve,* she reflected. It seemed he had not yet regained consciousness.

She looked around the private room for an empty vase. But blooms of every description decorated the room. She would take the carnations to Matron's office.

As she turned to go, the door opened and Nurse Gregory entered. Phyl Gregory ignored the younger girl completely. Penny merely shrugged her shoulders and walked out. She wasn't going to lose any sleep over Nurse Gregory's antagonistic attitude toward her. Penny had an idea that the beautiful staff nurse was keen on Don Anderson. As far as Penny was con-

16

cerned, the older girl was more than welcome to the E.N.T. consultant. The young surgeon was good fun, and in her own way Penny was quite fond of him. But for her there could never be anyone but Michael Ashmore. She had recognized that fact four years ago when she had been but a schoolgirl of fifteen.

Last year when her father was still alive, she had accepted the post as Dr. Ashmore's secretary in order to be near him. But much to her regret, their relationship had not advanced beyond the friendship stage. It was a deep, abiding friendship but only a friendship, Penny reminded herself with an inward sigh.

Yet a word from her and Don Anderson would come running. A little encouragement and Don might even ask her to marry him. Of that Penny was absolutely certain. Don adored her; he had said so many times.

Yesterday she had been quite sure he was about to propose to her. He had telephoned after lunch saying he was free for a few hours and that he would like to take her out somewhere. There was something important he wanted to ask her. But she, expecting to hear from Michael and fearful of missing him, had agreed to let the young surgeon visit her only if they remained at home.

It was just as well, Penny now told herself, that she and Don had not gone for a drive. There had been that emergency call from the hospital and the E.N.T. consultant had raced back to perform his brilliant surgery on the boy's ear.

Yes, Don Anderson was brilliant, sociable, and a gay companion. He was as tall as the medical superintendent though not quite so slim. Penny was well aware that the young nurses admired his dark, attractive looks. Perhaps she was a fool to let him slip out of her fingers.

A plan evolved in Penny's mind. Perhaps Michael would appreciate her better if she did take more notice of Don. A little competition would do Dr. Ashmore no harm, Penny decided with a little secret smile.

She hummed a happy tune as she continued to walk along the hospital corridors, Matron's carnations clutched in her hand.

CHAPTER THREE

"Michael, won't you kiss me good-by?" Penny's blue eyes were wistful. Her sweet lips were raised expectantly.

Dr. Ashmore hesitated. Then, inclining his head, he gently kissed the girl's forehead.

"Oh, Michael!" Penny voiced her disappointment. "That's not how you used to kiss me when I was little."

"But you're a child no longer," he reminded her half playfully.

"In some ways you treat me as if I were still a child." Penny looked and sounded hurt. "You're being illogical, and that's not like you, Michael."

The superintendent smiled tolerantly as he moved toward the window. Yesterday's cold breeze had turn to a strong and steady wind. Now heavy rain was causing visitors to scurry across the grounds toward the shelter of the hospital.

As a rule, Dr. Ashmore preferred his secretary to be an older, more mature woman. It was only in response to the late Henry Fielding's request that Michael had consented to let the young girl work for him at the hospital. In spite of an age difference of about twelve years, the great surgeon had been his best friend, and Michael sadly missed the older man's companionship.

At the time he had employed Fielding's daughter, the superintendent was not ignorant of the girl's devotion to him. He was aware of the great influence he had over her. At present he was not unduly concerned. In fact, he was slightly amused, perhaps even a little flattered. Penny was very lovely; she was sweet and generous, altogether a most delightful girl. Many of the young doctors were a little in love with her, Michael knew. But the young girl, lacking in vanity, was quite oblivious of this. It was a good thing, too, Dr. Ashmore decided.

This evening she had volunteered to work late. Now, the

pathological and medical reports, all neatly typed, were on his desk ready for his perusal.

Penny's voice caused Dr. Ashmore to turn from the window. "Why don't you kiss me the way you used to do?" With determination she pursued the subject.

"Because you're no longer a small girl. Please grow up, Penny!"

She bit her lip. "Is it that you think I'm not attractive enough to kiss?"

He stifled a yawn. "Of course not, you silly goose! You must reserve your kisses for the man you will one day love and marry. Your father would have wanted it that way. In a way, I'm endeavoring to guide you as your father would have done. I feel it my duty to do so. I'm old enough to be your father," Michael added teasingly. "Well — almost . . . ."

"You're not! You look years younger than your age, Doctor." Her eyes shone with admiration.

"Thank you, my pet. Now it's time I went to have some supper. And you must be getting home. You told me you had a date with Anderson this evening."

She grimaced. "What miserable weather."

"I find it invigorating."

"You would! I've a mind to phone Don and say I can't make it."

"You have your car, I suppose."

She nodded, buttoning her coat.

As she turned to leave, he called: "Penny — just a moment."

"Yes." She regarded the doctor expectantly. He was back at his desk; she stood at his side.

He glanced up at her with a quizzical smile. "Just a word of friendly advice. Whatever you do, don't play with Anderson's feelings. You'll regret it if you do."

"I've no intention of doing anything of the kind. I'm quite fond of Don, really I am. And he adores me."

"I wonder." Michael muttered the words under his breath.

"What was that?"

"Nothing. Merely thinking aloud." He paused. "I don't wish to discourage you, but please go carefully where Anderson is concerned."

A little ripple of laughter escaped her lips. "You sound very much like Miss van Ryhn now. That's how she would speak. Matron is so staid, so disapproving in many ways."

The gray eyes regarding the girl held a rebuke.

"Matron is a fine woman."

19

"Miss van Rhyn is a Christian," Penny reminded the doctor with a frown. "You seem to have forgotten that fact. And you have no time for Christianity. As a young girl I had the greatest respect for Ruth van Rhyn. But you took away some of that respect, Doctor."

"I?" He raised his brows in puzzlement.

"Yes. You did, Michael." Penny sat down.

He leaned back in his chair and crossed his legs. "How on earth did that come about? I'd like you to refresh my memory."

"You may not remember, but Ruth once took me to a Sunday school anniversary. I was about fourteen at the time. I thoroughly enjoyed the service. I had always wanted to attend Sunday school, but Father thought it was a waste of time, as you know. Ruth brought me home afterwards — she stayed to Sunday lunch. You were also present."

"Was I?" Dr. Ashmore appeared a little vague. "Can't say I can recall the occasion."

"But I can — vividly. You put some rather awkward questions to Miss van Rhyn — questions which I then thought she was unable to answer satisfactorily. But now, looking back, I guess she was too polite to argue. You asked whether she believed the Word of God. 'Most emphatically I do,' she replied. Then you began putting to her the usual questions most agnostics and atheists ask. Ruth replied that she didn't want to be drawn into any discussion about these matters, but that she was quite willing to have a little chat with you some other time should you wish it. She was back on duty directly after lunch, so there wasn't much time, anyway. Did you ever have that chat with her?"

"Not that I can recollect," the doctor rejoined absently.

"But you had a chat with me instead. How well I remember that talk! Up till then I had a vague belief in God, but you shattered that completely. Your views are now my views, Michael." Penny's eyes were filled with tender devotion.

He seemed taken aback. "But my views are not necessarily the right ones, Penny. You must think these things out for yourself."

"I am quite satisfied, Doctor. What you believe in, I believe to be the truth." Her voice was warm and confident.

His face grave, he rose to his feet. "But I may be grossly mistaken in my views. Besides, I can't ever recall trying to influence you into believing there is no God. It is quite true I

20

don't hold with Christianity. I doubt the Bible, I doubt whether there is a God. If I have unwittingly destroyed your faith in God, I'm sorry. Deeply sorry."

Penny rose and placed a hand on his shoulder. "Don't reproach yourself in any way, Michael. I'm proud to embrace your views on life and religion. You're an intellectual — a thinker. You must have given the subject a great deal of thought and study."

A feeling of shame — an emotion quite foreign to him — gripped the doctor. Apart from reading certain atheistic literature, he had not given the subject much thought. He had been too indifferent, too self-satisfied, too preoccupied with his work to delve very deeply into the age-old controversy of whether there was a Supreme Being. In certain intellectual circles it was the accepted thing to doubt the existence of God.

But he had gained the impression that Ruth van Rhyn had studied the subject carefully. A pity Penny had not accepted Matron's faith instead of his own skepticism. It did not seem right somehow that a fresh, lovely girl should not believe in the existence of God.

Gently he disengaged Penny's hand from his shoulder. Frowning, he began to pace the room. He would do anything now to undo the harm he had done. Perhaps Ruth van Rhyn could help.

"What's the matter, Michael?" Penny's sweet voice intruded. "Please don't worry on my account. I'm proud and happy to be an agnostic."

With great effort he managed to conceal his deep distress.

"Now I must be going," Penny went on. "I don't want to keep Don waiting too long. He's inclined to be impatient."

"And hot tempered and emotionally unstable."

"But an excellent surgeon," Penny reminded the superintendent.

"That's correct. I take off my hat to him where surgery is concerned. All the same, I'd like to see you team up with someone of a more balanced temperament."

Her smile was mischievous. "Someone like yourself, for instance?"

He smiled back. "I'm too old — much too old for a lively young girl like you. Well, good-by, my dear. Enjoy yourself. But remember my advice."

Thoughtfully, Penny walked out of the great building toward the car park. Why should Michael now express concern on learning that she held his agnostic views? And what had prompted him to caution her about becoming too friendly with the E.N.T. consultant? Did Dr. Ashmore really care? Was he at last beginning to feel a little jealous? She hugged the idea warmly.

As Penny drove out of the grounds, the rain lashed furiously against the windshield. Because of the fierce wind, she decided to drive along the main road in the direction of Claremont. At the bus stop the solitary figure of a man was waiting under the street light. His face appeared familiar. Penny looked again and saw that it was Clyde Maxwell, the house doctor.

She slowed down and opening the window, she called out: "I'm on my way home. Hop in if you're going to Claremont."

When she traveled along the main road, Penny had to pass the church where Ruth and Clyde worshiped regularly. No doubt the house physician was on his way to a meeting. When not on call, he usually took the opportunity to attend a service, Sunday or no Sunday, so she had heard from Matron, who did exactly the same herself.

"Thanks." With relief Clyde opened the car door. "It looks as if we're in for an early winter. Been working late, Miss Fielding?"

Penny nodded and let in the clutch. "Entirely my own fault. I spent part of the afternoon chatting to various patients. Mi — Dr. Ashmore doesn't mind, provided I finish my work. How is Robin getting on? He was sleeping when I peeped into his ward."

"He is making splendid progress, I'm glad to say. But he's not yet out of the woods."

She turned to the intern with a smile. "Won't you call me Penny? Everyone does."

"I'd be delighted. And you must call me Clyde. I appreciate very much your giving me a lift, Penny." He smiled warmly.

"I'm glad now I decided to travel along the main road instead of the drive. It can be pretty eerie along that route in a storm. I'm always a little nervous of a tree being uprooted or branches falling on the car. Do you drive, Clyde?"

"I have a license. But unfortunately I'm not often able to drive." He made no attempt to explain further.

Perhaps his car was out of order; maybe he couldn't afford to have it repaired. Penny had overheard Dr. Ashmore's remark that the intern was as "poor as a church mouse." She had not taken the words seriously.

"How do you like being on duty in the Casualty Ward?" Penny inquired with genuine interest.

"I enjoy the work. One sees life in Casualty. You have no idea how careless people can be until you've been on duty in Casualty. Traffic accidents are on the increase; then there are the work accidents, not to mention the road accidents caused by drunken drivers." Clyde hesitated. "I thoroughly enjoyed studying medicine. Your father helped me a great deal, Penny. He was one of the best."

A lump came into her throat. "I agree there. I miss him dreadfully, Clyde." She felt tears rising in her eyes.

"I'm sorry. I shouldn't have brought up his name. Please forgive me, Penny."

"That's all right." She smiled sweetly. "In a way I'm surprised that you should think so highly of him, considering Father was not a Christian."

Clyde was at a loss of a suitable rejoinder. So he asked: "Are you a believer, Penny?"

Suddenly she was ashamed to answer him. She drove on silently.

"It seems I have offended you."

She said impulsively: "Oh, no, you haven't, Clyde. You see, I'm not a believer."

"Then you're missing something." His voice sounded sad. "I've been a Christian for many years now." Clyde's voice took on a joyous note. "For me there is no other life but the Christian way of living. Pleasing the Lord means everything to me."

That's how Ruth van Rhyn would speak, Penny mused. But, strange to say, now she felt no annoyance. Instead she was slightly intrigued.

They had now reached the church. Penny found she would like to chat further with him, but there wasn't much time left.

She said quickly: "I'm not really an unbeliever. Well — not exactly. I think you would call me an agnostic."

Clyde experienced a sense of shock. Such a young, lovely girl an agnostic. He did not think she knew what she was saying.

Penny went on: "That's what Dr. Ashmore calls himself. But I haven't studied the subject like he has. One day I may."

"Then please study the matter with an unprejudiced mind. That is most important. Perhaps — " Clyde paused briefly, "you will allow me to help you."

"Thank you. I'll think it over," Penny told the young doctor with one of her lovely smiles.

He felt a quickening of his pulse. Reluctantly he opened the car door.

"I'm most grateful for the lift, Penny. Remember, if you are ever in any need of spiritual help, I'd be delighted to talk with you. That's a promise."

It was with a sense of regret that Penny drove away. She was sorry now that she had arranged to go out with Don tonight. But it was too late to telephone him to put him off. Already he must be on his way to meet her.

Her mind filled with conflicting emotions, she parked her car, hurried indoors and began to dress for the evening.

CHAPTER FOUR

Ruth van Rhyn looked up in pleasure as in response to her "Come in," the medical superintendent entered her office.

Outside, the rain was still pounding heavily against the windows, deluging the lawns and flowerbeds, sweeping across the asphalt car park.

Dr. Ashmore seated himself in the chair Matron indicated and stretched his long legs. A weary sigh escaped his lips.

"Anything bothering you, Michael?" Ruth asked in her clear, calm voice.

He nodded. "Yes, there is. But before we discuss my problem, I'd like to speak to you about the Radford boy. He is proving most difficult to handle, as you doubtless know. Staff Nurse Gregory is having a rough time with him."

"Yes. That's so." Matron looked equally concerned. "He seems to have taken a dislike to the girl."

"That's an understatement. To me it's a clear-cut case of mutual hostility."

"Staff Nurse is doing her best."

The superintendent smiled inwardly. Matron was always loyal to her staff.

"I've just come from his room. I found Staff Gregory shouting at the boy. No matter how much a nurse is provoked, she must learn to control her indignation."

"I must admit that at present she appears to be a little unstrung."

"Perhaps she's soon due for her annual leave?"

Ruth shook her head. "Not for some time. Poor Phyl Gregory! She seems to be losing weight. She's not at all her usual self."

Dr. Ashmore flashed Matron an inquiring glance.

"In a way I can sympathize with Phyl Gregory," Ruth murmered. "She is having some difficulty with her love life."

"H'm . . . ." The doctor sat silent. Then he asked: "Who is the young man?"

Matron hesitated before making a reply. "Don Anderson."

Michael's pale brows rose slightly, whether in surprise or annoyance, Ruth wasn't quite sure.

She went on, "But Anderson, it appears, is keen on Penny."

"Perhaps." Dr. Ashmore's reply was noncommittal. "He's out with Penny this evening."

"I know. And that's what is making Staff Nurse so miserable. She is genuinely in love with Anderson, I think."

"H'm . . . . All the same, as a good nurse, she should not let her personal problems affect her work. I've come to ask you to speak to her."

"As you wish." Matron spoke with some reluctance. Or was it with disappointment? Dr. Ashmore couldn't be sure.

Ruth thought: *Is Michael anxious in case Phyl should take Don away from Penny? But he has no cause to worry. That wouldn't break Penny's heart. She cares too much for Michael himself . . . .*

Matron stirred from her cogitations when the medical superintendent spoke. "Ruth, I'm somewhat concerned about Penny." He paused for a long moment. "As you doubtless are aware, I have always questioned the basis of Christian truth — the Bible. I have entertained doubts about God's validity. But now I'm disturbed — deeply disturbed. I find I have unwittingly imparted my unbelief, my skepticism, to Penny."

Ruth nodded sadly. "Yes. I am well aware of that. I have been aware of it ever since that Sunday five years ago when I brought her home after the Sunday school anniversary. If you had not scorned my faith so openly that day, I'm quite sure I could have influenced her thinking along spiritual lines."

A rueful smile touched the superintendent's lips. "Don't remind me! Penny reminded me of the unfortunate incident before going home this evening. I must confess I had completely forgotten about it." He hesitated, his face grave. "I'd do anything now to undo the damage I've done."

"The young are so impressionable," was Matron's rejoinder. "So please don't blame yourself too harshly. Perhaps if you had a little chat with Penny — "

He interjected with bitterness: "It's too late, I'm afraid. The harm has already been done. I doubt whether anything I can say now will be of any consequence. Penny has embraced my agnostic views. And she is proud of them." The doctor uttered a low groan.

"With God all things are possible." Ruth smiled confidently at Michael.

"You seem to have forgotten that I question the existence of God."

"Forgive my asking, Michael, but what made you become an agnostic?" Her tone was warm with an engaging hint of apology. "Some tragedy in your life? An unhappy love affair?" Ruth held her breath; her heart pounded uncomfortably.

He smiled dryly. "Nothing like that! I suppose like so many people I just drifted into that way of thinking. To my shame, I must confess I haven't even studied the subject deeply — if at all, for that matter."

"Perhaps you were unconsciously influenced by Penny's father."

"Maybe. But as far as I can recall, Henry Fielding and I never discussed religion. We were both too engrossed in discussing medicine and studying the latest surgical methods." Dr. Ashmore glanced at his watch. "I shouldn't be bothering you like this." He rose to leave.

"It's a pleasure," Ruth smiled. "Perhaps we could have tea together. I'll ring for some if you like."

"A good idea." He sat down again and let his eyes wander around the office. His gaze came to rest upon the bookcase behind Matron's desk. That reminded him of his true purpose in calling.

"I really came to see whether you had a book I could read relating to the subject we were discussing. Something that would help Penny," he added swiftly, avoiding Ruth's eyes.

"I have several such books." Ruth went to the bookcase.

"You seem to have studied the matter pretty thoroughly," he observed with some display of interest.

Ruth nodded happily. "I have. I myself was a skeptic. But that was years ago."

The doctor gave her a swift scrutiny. He made no comment.

"When I was a student nurse — when I was Penny's age, I too had doubts — grave doubts which caused me much distress. For a long time I floundered in uncertainty. But after much prayer and the reading of countless books, I found the Lord graciously revealing His truth to me. The Book of Jeremiah, chapter 29 and verse 13, reads, 'And ye shall seek me and ye shall find me, when ye shall search for me with all your heart.' I did just that. God answered prayer in a most remarkable way."

The doctor's somber expression gave no clue to his thoughts. She was surprised when he exclaimed: "In that case you might be able to help Penny."

Ruth shook her head with regret. "I doubt it. It would be better if you spoke to her instead. I've lost whatever influence I had over her. She wouldn't listen to me. Now, if you read the books, one at the time, that is — " Ruth smiled, "then you would be able to discuss the subject with her. And if ever you should come to change your views — "

"That's most unlikely," he interposed in a mocking voice. "I've no interest whatsoever in religion. In fact, if you value my friendship at all, I must ask you not to suggest such a thing again. I will never change my views. And that's final!"

His face set into stern lines. Once more he was the medical superintendent, authoritative and aloof.

Seating herself at her desk, Ruth fumbled with her pen, playing for time to control her feeling of disappointment. It was a welcome diversion when the maid arrived with the tea.

In silence Ruth set the cups and poured out the tea. The happy companionship which had begun to blossom between them had been cruelly nipped in the bud by Michael's words, perhaps would never have a chance to flower.

Relentlessly the wind continued to drive the rain against the windows.

Michael put down his cup. "Thank you, Ruth. Now I must be going." He spoke curtly.

Her eyes as they met his were cordial, yet he perceived the disappointment in their depths.

"Would you still care to read one of the books?" Ruth ventured, looking away from him.

He hesitated, his face remote, inscrutable. Then he nodded. "Yes. For Penny's sake, I must."

Ruth took out a small volume from the shelf. "This book deals with medical science and the Scriptures. It's fairly easy to read and most interesting. I found it so, anyway."

He smiled that elusive, sardonic smile of his. His eyes were guarded as he glanced down at the title.

"What nonsense is this?" he asked, frowning. But Ruth could see he was not annoyed.

"You go ahead and read, and you will discover for yourself the truth of the words." Ruth answered him gravely, but there was a twinkle in her eyes. "The Bible definitely predates modern medicine."

For a moment he regarded Ruth in frank disbelief. Then he bade her a brief "goodnight" and was gone.

In spite of his attitude, there was joy in Ruth's heart. Was the Lord at long last about to answer prayer?

CHAPTER FIVE

"You look absolutely stunning! You're the most adorable girl I know."

Penny smiled in amusement. She was used to Don Anderson's extravagant way of speech.

All the same, she should feel flattered. The hospital grapevine had it that several of the nurses had lost their hearts to him. The E.N.T. consultant was all that a girl could desire – a brilliant surgeon, charming, vital, with dark, attractive looks. He was also gay and extravagant, which the medical superintendent was not. But unfortunately Don Anderson was given to sudden outbursts of temper. So far Penny had not had occasion to witness these displays of temper, so she couldn't quite understand Dr. Ashmore's concern at times.

Last week, in spite of the rain, she had enjoyed herself with Don. That was why she had allowed herself to be persuaded to go out with him again this evening.

Now the weather had cleared. The wind had dropped, the clouds had disappeared. The moon rode in solitary splendor in the midnight blue sky above.

Don took her arm in a possessive gesture and led her toward his car. An odd smile lurked on his lips.

"I've booked a table at that luxury restaurant on the Marine Drive. Ever been there?"

As Penny shook her head, Don went on: "Ever been out to a restaurant with the chief?"

"You know the answer to that one! When has Dr. Ashmore ever deigned to take a girl or woman alone to a restaurant? When Dad was alive, Doctor took us out occasionally. In my opinion he's too cautious, too much of a confirmed bachelor to be seen out alone with a girl. He can't stand gossip."

Don said significantly: "Old Ashmore is a dark horse. And so is Matron. The other evening on my way home from the hospital, I saw them together."

"You saw what!" Penny sounded startled. The color had ebbed from her face.

"I saw Ruth van Rhyn and our honored chief entering a restaurant together." There was a mocking light in Don's dark eyes.

Bravely Penny tried to summon a smile. "But — but what is so odd about that? No doubt they went there to talk shop. There is so much for them to discuss."

"I don't believe that one!" The hint of malice in Don's voice did not escape Penny.

"You don't exactly care for Dr. Ashmore, do you?"

"Quite frankly, I don't. But that's only because of you."

"Because of me?" Penny echoed with a grimace.

"Now don't look so innocent, my sweet one. It's common hospital knowledge that you're keen on the chief."

Penny's cheeks flamed. "I — I'd no idea people were talking."

"You're very transparent, my dear.

"Oh, Don! Why did you have to tell me? I feel awful now. You've completely spoiled my evening."

"Nonsense! I wouldn't let it bother me. Especially when it's not true. But is it, Penny?" he demanded. She felt the pressure of his hand on her arm.

She did not answer. He opened the car door for her to get in. He took his seat beside her.

"Is it?" he persisted, pressing his foot on the accelerator.

Penny's head went up. "I don't see that it's any business of yours, Don Anderson."

He affected a laugh. "Of course it's my business, you sweet darling. You're going to be the future Mrs. Don Anderson."

Penny giggled. "Don't be absurd! I've no intention of marrying you, Don."

"We won't talk about that now." His dark eyes held a strange glow. "What a gorgeous evening."

She made no comment. She sat silent and thoughtful as the E.N.T. consultant took the route along the Black River Parkway. Don's large car covered the distance with effortless ease and soon they were traveling along the Marine Drive.

Tonight the beauty of the sea with its mysterious shadows disturbed Penny profoundly. How often she had dreamed of coming here with Michael. But now that dream seemed more remote than ever.

Unconsciously she heaved a sigh. Don cast a swift glance at her profile. He saw that she was in the grip of an emotion in which despair and desire were mingled.

"Why so pensive? You're not on your way to a funeral, you know. You're going to dine and dance with me."

Resolutely Penny shook her head. "No dancing tonight, Don. I don't feel in the mood somehow."

Frustration rose within him. "Quite candidly," he observed scornfully, "I'd no idea you cared so much for old Ashmore."

"Michael's not old!" she retorted defensively. "And I don't like the way you keep referring to him as 'Old Ashmore.' He's not that old."

"Sorry." Swiftly Don veiled his expression. "But let's face facts. The chief's too old for you."

"Where did you see Doctor and Miss van Rhyn together?"

A guarded look leaped into Don's dark eyes. "At Sea Point."

"Sea Point?" Penny wrinkled her nose. "But you said you saw them together on your way home."

He pulled a wry face. "Quite the detective, aren't you? I first went home to change before driving out to Sea Point."

"Were you alone?" Penny pursued, not feeling in the least jealous.

With effort he crushed down his vexation. "I had Staff Gregory with me. Hope you are now satisfied, my sweet one."

"Not quite." Penny looked at him sharply. "What is there between you and Phyl Gregory?"

Don pulled the car to a standstill outside the restaurant. His hand rested lightly on Penny's shoulder.

"I don't know what you mean," he countered.

"Oh, yes, you do! You know very well what I mean. Phyl Gregory is in love with you."

"You don't say," he rejoined in mock surprise. "Well — what of it?"

"Aren't you encouraging her by taking her out?"

Not bothering to conceal his annoyance, Don glared at Penny. Then he shifted his gaze.

"Staff Nurse is an extremely lonely girl. She doesn't mix too easily. Her folk live upcountry. I'm merely showing her a little friendliness, that's all. Now, shall we go and have something to eat?"

32

The dimly lit lanterns decorating the restaurant gave the place an air of romance. Don smiled with satisfaction as he sat down opposite Penny.

"Smart place, this. We should come here more often."

She gazed about her uncertainly.

"How about a drink?" Don suggested eagerly.

"I'll just have a lemonade, thank you."

He smiled tolerantly. "Still refraining from liquor? Time you grew up, Penny. Have a sherry and judge for yourself — don't go by the chief's opinion."

She gave Don a direct glance .from her blue eyes. "Father never touched the stuff. He was too fine a doctor to do so. And you, as a medical man, should know that as well."

"My, my! You sound just like Matron now. But she's a Christian. And I know that you don't happen to approve of Christianity."

Penny appeared undecided. "I can't recall having said I don't approve of Christianity. A Christian must believe in God and in His Son, Jesus Christ. I'm not sure whether I believe in God. But surely there must be a Creator." There was a question in her voice. "Do you believe in God, Don?"

"Oh, yes!" the young surgeon rejoined at once. "I do believe in God. But I don't exactly hold with the Christian doctrine. Christians believe Jesus Christ to be a sort of Saviour from sin. But come, Penny, this conversation is getting too morbid. Now how about sampling a sherry with me?" He beckoned the wine steward.

"I'll have a lemonade, thank you," she retorted in a firm voice.

"Very well." Don failed to hide his chagrin. "I'll have a brandy, waiter."

"But, Don," Penny protested, "you're driving back."

"Well, what of it?" he demanded angrily. "I'm not some irresponsible teen-ager sampling my first drink. I can hold alcohol as well as any man."

Penny's eyes didn't waver before the blaze of his. "Dr. Ashmore was telling me this morning of a book he's reading. He's always been against alcohol. But now, as a medical man, his views have been strengthened considerably by the contents of this book. Strong drink is a robber, it says. Every year hundreds are killed by this evil on our drives and parkways. Alcohol produces a sort of atrophy in the brain — "

"I know all about that, my sweet one." Don's lips twisted

derisively. "I'll have you to know that I, too, have studied the subject."

Penny frowned. Her blue eyes were perplexed. "Then why persist in drinking? If it's harmful — and you admit it is — then why continue taking the stuff? It doesn't make sense to me."

"Don't be so naive, my dear. Why should I leave off taking something that makes me extremely happy?"

She sniffed in disdain. "The lift-up that lets you down. Alcohol is like a drug. You may feel happy now. Tomorrow you'll have a hangover."

"Not me!" was Don's proud boast. "Alcohol can't harm me."

"That's what you think! But Dr. Ashmore knows otherwise. He has studied the subject more intensely than you have. He knows the harm it can cause the body. What about the hardening of the liver, not to mention the number who die from delirium tremens? And you like the stuff!" There was disgust in Penny's voice.

Don's face grew red. The conversation was getting out of hand. He put on his most disarming smile.

"Come on, Penny. Now drink your lemonade like a good girl."

She appeared not to notice his sarcasm. Her thoughts had returned to Michael dining with Ruth van Rhyn.

Penny didn't feel very hungry. She merely toyed with her food. Don glanced at her questioningly.

"Why so thoughtful? Don't tell me you've still got the evils of alcohol on your mind?"

"Just where did you see Dr. Ashmore and Matron together?"

"Really, Penny!" Don put down his knife and fork. "You are the limit! Here you should be enjoying yourself with me — not discussing Ruth van Rhyn and the chief. Let's forget them."

"But there can't be anything between them — there just can't." Despair rose in her voice.

"Of course there isn't!" Don hastened to assure her, quickly veiling his exasperation. "As you've already mentioned, most probably they were out to discuss hospital matters. They've a great deal to talk over. Now cheer up and let me see your smile. You have a lovely smile, Penny."

She managed a smile.

"That's better. A grave face doesn't become you."

"Don — tell me — what do you think of Miss van Rhyn?"

"What do I think of Matron?" Don frowned.

"Please! I'd like your opinion."

"What a persistent young lady you are. I'd never have thought so. Why such sudden interest in dear Matron?"

"I've always been interested in Ruth. Well — sort of," Penny amended quickly. "I've known her since I was a child. In fact, I've known her for as long as I've known Michael — and that's a good many years now. She's always struck me as being disinterested in men."

"Don't you believe it! What woman is not interested in men, I'd like to know."

"Do you like her, Don?" Penny's eyes were on his face.

He nodded briefly. "I do. She's a good sort. I've got no complaints. Most of the doctors and surgeons like her. She's rather goodlooking."

"Oh." A pause. "Do you think that perhaps Dr. Ashmore likes her as well?"

Don laughed. "My dear girl, how should I know? I've not given it a second thought. Maybe he does — maybe he doesn't. Pity I haven't a daisy chain with me."

"Now you're teasing me." Penny sounded aggrieved.

Don's face sobered. "On the whole, I have an idea he does like her. Previously he was merely indifferent to her. But now — "

Eagerly Penny waited for the E.N.T. consultant to continue.

"I think I'm correct in assuming that he's just recently begun to take notice of her."

"What makes you say that?"

"Really, Penny!" Don was fast losing his patience. "I take you out to dinner and all you can talk about is the chief and Matron. Can't you change the subject?"

Penny flushed. He noticed with quick remorse the shadow of pain in her eyes.

She was silent for a few minutes while Don continued eating. Then she ventured: "Ruth seems quite friendly with our young house doctor."

"Matron merely lifts him to church. The poor beggar can't afford a car yet."

"Is he that poor?" Penny's question was filled with sympathy. "Then how did he manage to go through medical school?"

Don shrugged. "I've heard rumors that his family left him a small legacy. No doubt his sister helped him as well. She's some years older than he is."

"His sister has recently married. She's the new Mrs. Radford."

Don nodded. "I know that. An attractive-looking woman. She deserves a break. A pity about her stepson."

"No doubt everything will iron itself out in time. Robin only needs time to adjust himself to his new circumstances."

"You see a lot of Robin. He seems to have taken a fancy to you."

Penny smiled fondly. "Perhaps it's a good thing. He and Phyl Gregory don't appear to hit it off too well. Staff Nurse doesn't like me either."

The surgeon made no comment. Quickly he reverted to the subject of Clyde Maxwell.

"Now that's a young fellow I can really admire."

"You can?" Penny eyed Don with interest.

"Yes. I'm fair enough to give credit where credit is due."

"That's nice of you, Don." There was a note of respect in her voice.

"Not at all — not at all." Don warmed to his subject. At last it seemed he had captured Penny's regard. Old Ashmore wasn't going to have it all his own way much longer. A little more perseverance and soon Penny would be gazing at him with the same rapt admiration that she gave the chief.

Deliberately he refrained from ordering another brandy.

"Yes, our young intern certainly has the makings of a very fine doctor. He should go far. I dare say you know he's rather religious. Perhaps I should say very."

"Is he? But so is Matron. No doubt that's why they're so friendly."

"You sound disappointed." Don gave her a sharp glance.

Penny laughed. "Now don't misunderstand me. I think I'd have preferred it if they were friendly for other reasons."

"But there's a difference of some ten years between them, if I'm not mistaken."

"I know." Penny sighed. "I wish you hadn't told me you'd seen Ruth with Michael."

"But it's better that you should know the truth," Don pointed out. "The chief isn't quite so immune to a woman's attentions as you seem to think."

She resented the criticism in Don's voice.

"Not for a moment do I believe Ruth is chasing Michael. And I doubt whether she cares for him in any special way."

"She's fond of him, all right." Don leaned across the table to take Penny's hand. "And he of her for that matter. Perhaps more than he will admit, even to himself. But why bother with them? Ashmore is not for you. Now, you're my girl." His eyes upon her were dark, inscrutable.

"Don, please — " She pulled her hand away. "Please take me home." The mysterious gleam in his eyes made her a little afraid.

"And brood? What do you take me for? Do you imagine I'd leave you like this? We're going for a long drive, you and I." He caught her hand in an ardent squeeze.

This time she made no protest. Don was right. Why should she go home and brood?

They drove for a long time in silence. Don had no intention of giving Penny up to Dr. Ashmore. She was so truly feminine, so delightful. Not chic, not glamorous, but sweet and unsophisticated. Not exactly his type — Don shrugged mentally. But Penny was wealthy, and wealth to him was the gateway to success. And that he wanted more than he wanted any woman — even Phyl Gregory.

CHAPTER SIX

The telephone at the E.N.T. surgeon's bedside trilled plaintively.

Don Anderson yawned loudly as he lifted the receiver to his ear.

"Hullo!" He spoke curtly. "Anderson here."

A woman's voice came uncertainly over the line.

"Don — it's me — Phyl — "

"Phyl!" he exclaimed sharply. His heavy scowl betrayed his anger. "What do you mean by waking me up at this unearthly hour on a Sunday morning? You know I hate to be disturbed. I should have let the phone ring."

"It might have been an emergency call from the hospital."

"Well, it's not! And now I'm hanging up. Good-by!"

"Don — wait! I must talk to you." Phyl was unsuccessful in keeping the agitation out of her voice.

"Not now, for heaven's sake. I'm still half asleep."

"It's well after nine o'clock. You can't be that sleepy." A pause. Then: "You were out last night with Penny Fielding." There was an underlying note of accusation in Phyl's voice.

"What of it?" he demanded angrily. "I wish you'd mind your own business."

"But it is my business, Don. We love each other."

"Speak for yourself — "

"Oh, Don — "

"That's enough! It's all over between us — finished! Now please get off the line. By the way, from where are you phoning?"

"The hospital — "

"Good grief, girl! Haven't I told you not to ring me from Oakhurst unless it concerns a case? You never know who might be listening. Now let me get some sleep."

38

"I must talk to you, Don. When can I see you? I'm off duty this afternoon from two until five."

The pause was so long that Staff Nurse Gregory thought the surgeon had rung off. Then his voice came harshly over the line.

"Now listen here, Phyl. There's nothing left to discuss. We had everything out on Thursday evening, remember?"

Phyl found she could not speak. The memory of it still stung. It hurt so much that even now she felt tears prick her eyes.

She had been absolutely stricken when he'd told her it was all over between them, and had protested, "But I can't let you go like this. What do you take me for? I love you, Don." It was the first time she had ever pleaded with a man. "And you love me, too. You can't deny it. How can I let you go after all we've meant to each other? You don't mean a thing to Penny Fielding. You never will. She's keen on the chief. Can't you see that you're wasting your time?"

"Now listen here, Phyl!" Don's eyes, which previously had looked at her with such admiration, had blazed with anger.

In desperation she had caught hold of his sleeve. She had not thought that the time would come when she, beautiful and desirable — so Don had frequently declared — would have to plead for a man's love. From the very first day she and the E.N.T. surgeon had met, his eyes had told her that he wanted her and he had lost no time in seeking her out to court her.

"I warn you," he had said early in their courtship, "I'm horribly extravagant and up to my neck in debt." Don was an ardent racegoer and so far he had lost heavily on the races, but he still clung to the belief that one day he would win a fortune.

"When my debts are paid, then you and I will be married, my darling Phyl. At present I can't afford a wife. Even my car isn't paid for — "

"I don't mind at all, darling — honestly I don't. I'll continue with my nursing after we're married — "

He had silenced her with a passionate kiss. "I wouldn't like a wife of mine to work. What do you think the hospital staff will say? No, my darling, we'll just have to wait."

She had frowned. Her voice was anxious. "But for how long? I'd like us to be married while I'm still young. As things are at present, we might have to wait for years yet. No, Don. I'm determined to work. Not here at Oakhurst — I'll do private nursing. The pay will be better. But please don't ask me to wait — I may meet someone else," she had added teasingly.

He had taken her in his arms and crushed her to him. "You're my girl. Let's consider ourselves engaged. But secretly, mind you."

And so they had continued to see each other regularly in their off-duty hours, until a few months after Henry Fielding's death.

The great surgeon was the only one who knew of their secret engagement. One afternoon he had accidentally discovered Don Anderson and Staff Nurse Gregory embracing passionately in the deserted operating theater. Frowning his disapproval, he had scolded the couple severely for their unethical behavior. However, when he was told of their engagement, he had accepted their apologies; he had even permitted himself a smile and had wished them every happiness.

That was why, when on Thursday evening she and Don had met, she had remarked with bitterness: "If Fielding were still alive, you wouldn't dare try to court his daughter. He knew about us, remember?"

"Be quiet!" the young surgeon had shouted with mounting fury. "Can't a fellow change his mind? For the last time let me tell you it's all over between us. Finished!"

Almost distraught, she had cried: "But you can't possibly love Penny Fielding! You hardly know her. Besides, she's such a child. She's so dreadfully young for her age."

"I intend to marry her all the same." Don's eyes were gleaming with determination. "And you're not going to stop me, Phyl. No one is. Not even old Ashmore. Perhaps you're right — I may not love her — well, not in the way I loved you. But there are other things besides love — far more important things. I'm ambitious. Money is the gateway to success. Penny's money can help me."

As the implication of his words penetrated, Phyl was frankly appalled. "You can't mean you're marrying the girl for her money. Oh, Don! Not that! You'll regret it if you do."

The E.N.T. surgeon laughed and shrugged his shoulders. "That's my affair. I'm surprised that you're so squeamish about such things. You're no saint, my girl."

She stiffened. "But I draw the line when it comes to marrying for money."

As he saw the pained expression in her eyes, he knew an impulse to take back the hurtful words he had spoken.

"Look here, Phyl. Let's be sensible about this. We've had some grand times together. Perhaps I still love you — I don't know.

40

At the moment I must confess I'm somewhat confused. Anyhow, as things are at present, we can't be married for years.

"If you left off betting on those wretched horses we could. In spite of everything, I'd still marry you, Don. I'm prepared to work — "

He had intervened with a mocking smile. "Such touching devotion. I don't deserve it, my dear."

She had ignored his sarcasm. In desperation she had caught hold of his sleeve. "Oh, Don, I love you so much. Don't give me up. Deep down in your heart you still love me. Even now when one of your colleagues happens to notice me, you still show signs of resentment. Don't deny it. You'll be sorry if you let me go — "

"But I must, Phyl! I must!" His voice sounded desperate. "Don't you see? One day I'll want my own practice. Penny's money can help me — "

With irony, the staff nurse interrupted: "What good is money if it doesn't bring you any happiness? You're not Penny's kind — she couldn't make you happy. Oh, I admit she's sweet. But so immature. She's still playing at life and love. She's had an easy life — not like me. Besides, she's devoted to the chief — everyone knows that."

"That's enough said. I'm marrying Penny and that's all there is to it."

"Has she agreed to marry you, then?" With an effort Phyl had disciplined her voice.

"No. We haven't discussed marriage yet."

Phyl had laughed scornfully. "You'll have the chief to contend with."

Don had sniffed. "What's old Ashmore got to do with it? He'd better mind his own business and not try to interfere. The same as I'm asking you, Phyl. Now let me drive you home."

That had been Thursday evening. Last night Don had been out with Penny again. Phyl could no longer contain herself. She just had to find out whether the young girl had consented to marry the man she herself loved so hopelessly.

Her voice came frantically over the line. "Are you still there, Don?"

But he had already rung off. For a few moments Phyl was unable to move. Then, mustering all her professional composure, she forced her legs to carry her back to the boys' ward where she was on duty.

She smiled mechanically at Matron. But her smile did not conceal the anguish in her eyes.

Ruth flashed the staff nurse a sympathetic smile.

Matron is really a dear, Phyl decided, and had an overwhelming impulse to confide in her. But the staff nurse crushed down the desire and walked over to a young patient's bed. Picking up his chart, she studied with deliberate concentration the boy's temperature, pulse and respiration.

Satisfied that all was in order, she replaced the chart and stood absently looking down at the child.

The ward door swung open. A medical orderly and a junior nurse wheeled in a young patient. The staff nurse helped them to place the boy, who was still under the anesthetic, in the bed that had been prepared for him.

Next moment Dr. Ashmore entered. He had just performed a somewhat tricky appendectomy. The diagnosis had been acute appendicitis, but unfortunately peritonitis had set in.

Walking straight over to the boy's bedside, the medical superintendent felt his pulse. Then, not looking at Phyl, he said: "Staff Nurse, please prepare for the intravenous infusion. A house surgeon will be along presently to fix up the dextrose and saline drip."

"Very good, Doctor," Phyl rejoined with professional politeness.

As Dr. Ashmore turned to leave, he smiled across the ward at Matron. And as usual, Ruth's heart filled with song.

Resolutely she cast Michael from her mind and continued to move around the ward, stopping a moment or two at the various bedsides to smile cheerily at the young patients, here and there giving an encouraging word.

When she came to where the new patient was sleeping, Ruth glanced across the bed and met the eyes of the staff nurse. Phyl's pale face reflected her inward grief.

Ruth longed to comfort the staff nurse, to assure her that Penny was not seriously attracted to Don Anderson, and that in time she would tire of his attentions. A little patience and Don would be hers again.

As Ruth came out of Robin Radford's room, she met Clyde in the corridor. Warmly they smiled at each other.

"Robin seems much brighter this morning. He'll soon be ready to go home."

Clyde shook his head and said earnestly: "Leonora and Colin have agreed to let him remain here a few days longer. Robin is still rebellious at heart, I'm afraid. In my spare time I've been reading a few Bible stories to him. But so far there's been little response, if any."

"H'm." Ruth was looking thoughtful. "I wonder — "

Clyde smiled. "What's on your mind?"

"Penny. . . ."

"Penny?" the house doctor repeated in a subdued voice. "You can't mean Penny Fielding?"

Ruth nodded. "I do. She would be the ideal one to read to Robin. She gets on famously with children. I'll suggest it to her and see what she says."

"I doubt whether Miss Fielding will agree. Not to reading Bible stories, anyway. She told me — " Disconcerted, the intern broke off.

Ruth's eyes held a question. Clyde went on: "One evening last week she gave me a lift to church. It was raining hard that Wednesday, remember? I was waiting at the bus stop. She stopped and offered me a lift which I accepted gratefully. Really decent of her," he ended with an embarrassed gesture.

Matron smiled fondly. "Penny is a dear. I'm quite confident she'll only be too pleased to read to Robin. No doubt she mentioned to you that she was an agnostic?"

"She did. It's a disturbing thought. A young, sweet girl holding such dreadful views."

"Yes, it is sad. She's been influenced by Dr. Ashmore, I'm afraid. Reading Bible stories to the boy will do her a world of good. And Robin as well."

"Not if she puts across her own interpretation of the stories," the house doctor countered, looking perturbed at the thought. "In that case she'll do more harm than good."

"You need have no fears on that point, Clyde," Matron assured him. "Penny is a highly impressionable girl. Once she starts reading the stories, she'll forget her own point of view, or rather, Dr. Ashmore's. So far I have been unsuccessful in getting her to read a single book or to attend a service with me. But things are gradually changing, Clyde. I have every confidence that soon the Lord will answer prayer." Ruth's eyes held a wonderful serenity.

"You mean as regards Miss Fielding?" The intern asked with interest.

Ruth hesitated. Clyde wondered at her heightened color.

"In a way. But it's the chief I'm thinking of primarily. He's been reading a book on medical science in relation to the Bible. Doctor is greatly impressed. If he should come to know the Lord, it wouldn't be long before Penny puts her trust in Him, too."

"That would be grand," Clyde concurred with enthusiasm.

"Now I must be getting along." Matron gathered up her cloak. "By the way, will you be free to come to church this evening? I'll meet you as usual at the car park about seven o'clock."

The intern nodded. "Thanks, Ruth." He smiled. "That's the one and only thing I've got against this profession. I'm not often able to attend church twice on a Sunday. See you later then."

With an abstracted air, Clyde stood for a moment and watched Matron walk away.

A sweetly smiling face rose before him.

With determination he thrust the image aside and opened the door to Robin's room.

CHAPTER SEVEN

Entering her office, Ruth switched on the transistor radio. Occasionally when she was on duty she had a chance to listen to the church broadcast.

There were still fifteen minutes before the service began, so Ruth pulled out the book the medical superintendent had returned to her last night.

She had been thrilled when on Thursday evening he had suggested they go out together. At five o'clock, just as she was going off duty, Dr. Ashmore had approached her.

"I find I'm not on call this evening. How about having dinner with me, Ruth? I'd like to discuss with you that book you loaned me. I find it fascinating — absolutely astounding. I had no idea these scientific facts were to be found in the Bible."

For a moment she had been too stunned with joy to speak. It was like some glorious dream come true — Michael asking her to dine with him, but much more important, Michael, the agnostic, reading a book relating to God's Word. And enjoying it so much!

Dr. Ashmore had frankly admitted that his only motive in reading the book had been to help Penny. But as he had read on, he found himself becoming engrossed in the book for his own sake. As a doctor he found the contents invaluable.

"I'd like a copy for myself," he had told Ruth, his eyes earnestly meeting hers across the table. Her eyes glowed with pleasure and he thought how attractive she looked this evening in aquamarine blue. The rich color suited her admirably and he wondered again how all these years he could have been unaware of her as a woman. Until recently, to him she had been merely part of the hospital equipment. But now —

The medical superintendent halted in his cogitations. He had always had an aversion to becoming emotionally involved with a woman. He didn't really want to get married. His single state was his by choice. He reveled in his freedom and he definitely did not intend to marry.

But, he told himself, friendship with Ruth van Rhyn was an entirely different matter. He doubted, anyway, whether she would even consider matrimony. The hospital was her life, her career, the same as it was his. No, not her life, he reminded himself. God was her life, her whole world — she lived only to please Him. In helping suffering humanity she was serving God.

Matron's voice invaded his reflections. "Does that mean you now believe in God?" Her eyes were alive with interest.

He shrugged his slim shoulders. "That's a somewhat difficult question to answer. I'd rather not commit myself."

As she did not speak, he went on: "Unlike the atheist, at no time have I ever denied the existence of a Supreme Being. Now, in the face of the evidence in this book, I have to admit the possibility of a Creator. In fact, I'd go so far as to say that there is a God."

Ruth nodded happily. "Everything in nature points to that indisputable fact. Science proves beyond all doubt that God designed and created the universe. Just think of the evidence we have. You know that the earth rotates on its own axis at one thousand miles per hour. If it rotated only at one hundred miles, our days and nights would be ten times as long as they are now, and the earth would alternately burn and freeze. Then again, the sun has a surface temperature of twelve thousand degrees F. and our earth is at the exact distance from it to get just enough heat that it needs and not too much. I could go on and on, but I think that's enough for the time being," and she smiled radiantly across the table at her companion.

Michael marveled at the transformation in Ruth. Her face was alive, animated. She looked ten years younger. In spite of himself, he found her enthusiasm communicating itself to him.

Dr. Ashmore's natural reserve and caution were flung to the wind as he remarked: "What impressed me most in that book was the chapter about the washing of the hands. As you are aware, today no surgical procedure is performed without meticulous scrubbing of the hands. Epidemics and an unnecessary loss of lives have resulted from improper washing of the hands. Before the twentieth century the mortality from surgery was appalling. When in the middle of the nineteenth century a young surgeon instituted the washing of hands, he was laughed out of court. So up again went the mortality rate, and all because of prejudice against the washing of hands."

"If only doctors and surgeons had heeded the injunction in Numbers 19 which God gave to Moses regarding the safest method of cleansing the hands, all this needless loss of lives could have been avoided." Ruth paused and looked directly at the medical superintendent. "That's one reason why I said that God's Word predates modern medical science."

He nodded thoughtfully. "Maybe you're right. Then, if the Bible is true, I must believe in God, the Creator of the Universe. Logically I have no option but to believe. And yet — "

"You are finding it difficult, I know." Ruth spoke sympathetically. "It was the same with me. But the discovery comes by revelation. We may have a head knowledge of Him without a heart knowledge. This revelation comes by trusting the Lord Jesus Christ, God's Son, as one's own personal Saviour."

Michael's smile was a trifle sceptical. "Yes, somehow I knew you would lead up to this. That is the Christian's Gospel — salvation through faith in God's Son. I am acquainted with that doctrine," he added, meeting her inquiring glance. "My mother was a believer, you'll be glad to know. She died when I was in my teens. I was very fond of my mother and in my heart I blamed God for taking her from me."

Ruth's heart went out to him in compassion. She could well understand a sensitive young boy becoming disillusioned through the loss of a loved one. It happened often.

Even now, at the age of 38, he still looked embittered and unhappy, but also a little pensive. In spite of his poise and control and seeming haughtiness, there was about him an aura she had not been quite able to pinpoint and which she had often wondered about. Now she knew. It was that little lost boy look which had first drawn her to him.

Unconsciously her hand went out to his across the table.

"I'm sorry, Michael."

The warm pressure of her hand was somehow reassuring. It evoked within him a variety of feelings. Consolation, hope, a sudden desire to know God — a longing for true affection. He could not say which feeling predominated. He found his emotions difficult to analyze.

47

She let his hand go and said: "I must give you a Bible to read when we get back to the hospital."

He made no comment. His glance was doubtful, even a little suspicious. He felt as if the control of his life were being abruptly wrenched out of his hands and given to another.

Conversation on the return journey was impersonal and sparse. Once more he was the medical superintendent, cool and detached.

Undaunted by his attitude, she prayed inwardly that he would accept her offer. When they reached the hospital gate and Michael asked, without embarrassment, for the loan of a Bible, her heart was filled with gratitude and joy to the Lord for answering prayer.

Now, sitting at her desk and waiting for the broadcast service to begin, she wondered how Michael was progressing with the reading of God's Word. Apart from discussing hospital routine, they had not spoken to each other since Thursday night.

The hymn which came clearly over the air was one of Ruth's favorites.

> To God be the glory! great things He hath done!
> So loved He the world that He gave us His Son,
> Who yielded His life an atonement for sin,
> And opened the life-gate that all may go in.

Absorbed in the words of the grand hymn, Ruth did not hear the soft knock on the door. She failed to hide her surprise when the medical superintendent stepped into her office.

Without speaking, he seated himself and appeared to listen intently.

In the pause that followed, he remarked: "We're not so busy at the moment. I have a few minutes to spare. I feel inclined to sit here and listen with you — that is, if you have no objections, Ruth.'

Her earnest smile was tinged with something he was unable to define.

"Of course not! Please do stay, Michael."

The minister spoke on the great love chapter in I Corinthians 13, using the Amplified Bible. "Love endures long and is patient and kind; love never is envious nor boils over with jealousy; is not boastful or vainglorious, does not display itself haughtily. It is not conceited . . . it is not rude . . . it is not touchy or fretful or resentful . . . it takes no account of the evil done to it — pays no

48

attention to a suffered wrong. It does not rejoice at injustice and unrighteousness, but rejoices when right and truth prevail."

"God's Word declares that love is the fulfilling of the law. 'Thou shalt love the Lord thy God with all thy heart.' Many of our modern ills can be traced directly to the breaking of the laws found in God's Word. Resentment, anger, bitterness, hatred, envy, jealousy . . . all these deadly emotions have their repercussion on the human body. Countless people have sleepless nights brooding over their resentments. The advice of our Lord, 'Love your enemies,' may be ridiculed by many. But this advice is sound medically as well as spiritually. The Great Physician was thinking of our bodies as well as our souls when He uttered these words. The penalty of giving way to anger, to jealousy, to trying to get even with our enemies can bring on heart attacks, raise our blood pressure. Constant emotional turmoil can be the cause of numerous diseases."

Ruth and Michael nodded simultaneously at each other. Both were thinking of old Mr. Legg, whose blood pressure rose alarmingly every time he had a heated argument with a fellow patient. In spite of the fact that the irascible old gentleman could not afford a private room, arrangements were being made to have him removed to one. "He causes strife and bitterness wherever he goes," a relative had asserted without exaggeration.

The voice over the air continued: "Some modern psychologists would have us to believe that self is basically good and only needs educating. But the Word of God clearly states that in us 'dwelleth no good thing.' We all need regeneration. Our Lord said: 'Ye must be born again.' By sheer will power some may be successful in repressing these soul-destroying emotions. In Colossians 3:8, 9, we are told to put off anger, wrath, malice, evil speaking, lying. But to do this is impossible in our own strength. For a while we may to some extent succeed in subduing them, but in no time these ugly emotions begin to raise their heads. Only the Lord Jesus can deal with these sins — He who came to destroy sin by suffering anguish and death upon the Cross of Calvary for our sins. In that great Sermon on the Mount recorded in Matthew 5, our Lord said: 'Love your enemies and pray for those who persecute you.' These words are sound both spiritually and medically."

Ruth nodded approvingly. She was surprised when Michael exclaimed: "I'm inclined to agree with the preacher. He is quite correct in what he says. Emotional disturbances can play havoc with our health. We've both seen it happen many times. Retaliation is a disease producing emotion and brings in its wake insomnia. To harbor resentment and anger against a fellow being certainly destroys peace of mind." He spoke with unconcealed eagerness — an eagerness alien to his nature. "Therefore to love our enemies is good, sound advice."

Ruth's face was shining with delight. At long last, it seemed, light was beginning to dawn in Michael's soul. It wouldn't be long now, she reflected joyfully, before he would be able to state with complete assurance that the Lord was alive — that He lived within his heart.

"Ruth," Dr. Ashmore began hesitantly, so unlike his confident self, "may I accompany you to church this evening? You're off duty after five — and so am I."

"That would be lovely, Michael." There was praise and wonder in her heart.

"Good." He sounded highly satisfied. "We'll go in my car then."

"Oh dear, I'd almost forgotten. I've arranged to take Clyde Maxwell. He can borrow my car or maybe we can all go together. Whatever you suggest."

Dr. Ashmore rose to his feet. "We'll discuss that later."

The telephone shrilled demandingly. Matron picked up the receiver. She listened for a moment, then turned to the medical superintendent. "It's Casualty. A severe accident case has just been admitted and Maxwell needs your advice."

"Very well. I'll go at once." For an instant Dr. Ashmore stood with his hand on the door handle, a strange gleam in his steel-gray eyes. "See you later, Matron."

After he had gone, she sat for a long while lost in reverie.

CHAPTER EIGHT

"Dr. Maxwell." Clyde, on duty in the Casualty Department, paused momentarily as a young probationer approached him. "Matron would like to see you in her office as soon as you go off duty."

"Thanks." He smiled encouragingly at the nervous young girl. "Tell Matron I'll be along presently."

The student nurse hurried away, thinking what a nice young doctor Clyde Maxwell was.

Clyde looked down at the patient stretched out on the examination table. Gingerly he felt the man's leg.

"We'll soon have that wound fixed up. It's not as deep as it appears on the surface. A few stitches are necessary, though. In future, keep away from vicious dogs. You could have been severely bitten."

"It was the dog's fault," the patient complained in a belligerent voice. He shuddered again at the memory of the attack. "People should keep their beastly dogs chained up if they're vicious. They should keep them behind walls too high for the dog to jump over. I just stopped to pick a grape off the trellis, and before I knew what had happened the dog had got his teeth into me. And just because of one little grape . . . ."

"It was stealing all the same," the doctor interposed a little grimly. "It makes no difference in God's sight — one little grape or a dozen bunches. The intention to pilfer was there. Nurse, please prepare an anti-tetanus injection." Mentally Clyde made a note to hand the patient a tract before he went off duty.

Putting the last stitch in place, the intern straightened his back. "Nurse, the hypodermic, please."

The nurse obediently handed the doctor the syringe, then

carefully she swabbed the patient's arm. He scarcely felt the cold sharp run of the needle under his skin.

Clyde handed the syringe back to the nurse, who immediately dislodged the needle and placed it into the boiling sterilizer.

Ruth was waiting for the house physician as he entered her office.

"It's about this evening, Clyde. I shall be going to church with Dr. Ashmore." Clyde detected suppressed excitement in her voice.

He raised his brows in frank surprise. "Have I heard aright? You're actually going with the chief to church!"

Ruth smiled happily. "It's simply wonderful the way God works. You know I loaned Doctor that book about medical science in relation to the Scriptures. He fairly scoffed at the idea that the Word of God had anything to say about medical science. He read the book solely to help Penny, of that I'm quite certain. It's my opinion he has a guilt complex about her — he feels himself partly responsible that she has adopted his agnostic beliefs."

"It's a pity about that," and Clyde gravely shook his head. "A young girl like Penny practically denying the existence of God. It proves the tremendous power of influence. Such power over another certainly confers a serious responsibility." He paused. "Tell me, Ruth — if I'm not being inquisitive — what exactly is the chief's relationship with Penny Fielding? Hospital rumor has it that she's keen on him, and yet she is going out with Don Anderson. It doesn't make sense."

"Perhaps not. I know Penny admires Dr. Ashmore. Could be she even loves him."

"But the chief's so much older," Clyde protested with vigor. "Oh, I know Dr. Ashmore is a splendid man and I, too, admire him tremendously. All the same, he and Penny don't seem right for each other somehow. And as for Anderson — "

"Don Anderson is a different proposition," Ruth put in, "even though he is the younger man. No, I hardly think Penny will consent to marry him. She finds him good company — she is rather a lonely girl, you know. It may be that the younger doctors are somewhat diffident about offering to take her out. Remember, she is the late Henry Fielding's daughter."

Clyde appeared to consider the matter. "Should the chief become a believer, he may find it exceedingly difficult to alter her views about God," the intern remarked after a lengthy silence.

"Yes, that could be the case. But we mustn't lose sight of the

52

fact that with God all things are possible," Ruth reminded Clyde with a gentle smile. "Now about this evening. You may drive my car if you wish."

"Thanks, Ruth. It's a lovely evening for walking, so I'll just step it out tonight. A long walk will do me good. I need some fresh air after being on duty all day in Casualty."

"All right, then. But you are at liberty to come back with us in the car."

He smiled. "We'll see about that after the service. I'll pray as I stroll along that the chief will find the Lord tonight. Now I must go and change and see about supper before setting off to church. See you later, Ruth."

She smiled fondly at his retreating figure.

As Clyde had remarked to Ruth, it was a lovely evening. It was still early, dusk had not yet fallen, and the sky above was blue. He smiled reminiscently as he passed the bus stop where Penny had stopped to offer him a lift. She was so sweet, so utterly delightful. She did not look at all like an agnostic. There was about her no bitterness, no hardness. She was warm and affectionate, a light-hearted girl enjoying to the full the wonder of living. Perhaps at heart she wasn't really an agnostic. She had blindly embraced Dr. Ashmore's views regarding religion because of her high esteem for him. The question was: If Dr. Ashmore should become a Christian, how would it affect Penny?

Lifting his heart to his Heavenly Father in prayer, Clyde strode on with easy grace. He was oblivious of the roar of traffic as cars and buses hurtled passed him.

Glancing at his watch, he found he had covered the distance far more quickly than he had anticipated. The evening service began at 7:30, and as he had a half hour to spare, he decided to deviate from the main road and walked leisurely up a shady avenue, reveling in the peace and beauty that surrounded him. He was a lover of nature and paused for a minute to admire the sturdy oak trees arrayed in their autumn dress of russet and gold. Over a garden wall dahlias, decked in a variety of colors, proudly displayed themselves.

Suddenly a dog barked and the stillness was shattered. Almost simultaneously a car came speeding around the corner and abruptly jerked to a halt a few yards ahead of him. Clyde glanced down at the rear left wheel. A puncture. Then, looking at the car, he recognized it. Penny's car! Unexpectedly he knew a quickening of his pulse.

He was at her side in an instant. Her eyes lit up at the sight of him. "Clyde! How wonderful! Just when I need someone to help me change the tire. Oh! But I see you're all dressed up in your Sunday best. On your way to church, I presume?"

He nodded. "But it won't take me long to change that tire. I have time."

"But you'll get yourself all greasy — "

"Don't worry! I'll take care." Already he had taken off his jacket and placed it on the back seat of the car. Now he was rolling up his sleeves and asking her where the jack was kept.

Quickly Penny opened the trunk. Without speaking, Clyde took out the tools and some newspaper which he spread on the ground. In no time he had taken the flat tire off and was pumping up the spare.

With dawning admiration she watched him. How strong and steady were his hands. A pity about his being so poor that he couldn't afford to specialize. He'd make an excellent surgeon with that sure, steady control of his.

I like him . . . he is nice . . . much nicer than Don. But she couldn't very well use Clyde to make Michael jealous. It would seem cheap somehow.

Her eyes were warm with gratitude as he replaced the tools.

"Now be sure," he told her, "to take that flat to the garage tomorrow."

"Thanks, Clyde. I'll do that. Now you must come home with me to wash and brush up. By the way, Ruth van Rhyn on duty tonight?"

He shook his head. "She's gone with the chief to church."

In frank disbelief Penny stared at Clyde. "You mean to say she's gone with Michael Ashmore to church? But that's impossible!" Penny sounded slightly frantic, he thought. "You must be mistaken, Clyde. I just can't believe it. Michael wouldn't dream of attending church."

"It's an absolute fact, Penny."

"Then she must have persuaded him pretty hard."

Clyde said solemnly. "The Chief asked to go with Matron. He offered to take her to church."

"Oh, no!" Penny let out a dramatic cry. "This is getting worse and worse."

"Come on! Let me drive you home." Without further ado, the intern climbed into the driver's seat and let in the clutch.

54

"Oh, Clyde! It's bad of Ruth to try to take Michael away from me. But she won't succeed! I won't let her!"

Clyde glanced briefly at Penny, at the naked despair in her blue eyes. Her sweet lips were set in a mutinous line.

"Personally, I hardly think Ruth has even considered the idea. For some time now she has been concerned with the chief's spiritual welfare. I'm thrilled that at last he has volunteered to attend a service. There has been no persuading on Ruth's part, let me assure you. She has prayed for him, yes. But the chief wouldn't know about that."

Penny was silent. Clyde resumed: "I'd no idea there was an understanding between you and the chief."

She had the grace to flush. "There isn't, really," she admitted, "but I'm living in hopes. We got along famously when Dad was alive. But now Michael seems to be cooling off. I suspect Ruth has something to do with it. She's after him herself."

The intern shook his head in vigorous denial. "Penny, please don't misjudge Ruth. She wouldn't wittingly hurt another person. I happen to know her a little better than you do."

Penny seemed to ponder his words. She made no comment.

As he pulled the car to a standstill in the driveway, she said: "If you have time, would you mind coming back here for a short while after church?"

He showed his surprise. When he hesitated, she asked: "You're not on call later this evening?"

"No. Not until tomorrow morning. All the same — " Dubiously Clyde glanced at the girl, perceiving the wistful, rather unhappy expression in her eyes. Compassion stirred.

"All right — I'll come."

"Good." He wondered why she appeared so relieved. "Now you'd better hurry to wash your hands or you'll be late for church. There's a cloakroom downstairs you can use. I'll come for you after the service."

"That's all right," Clyde put in quickly. "It won't take me five minutes to walk up here. I'll see you about a quarter to nine."

He slipped into the church just as the choir members filed into their pews. On the right side of the aisle he saw Matron sitting with his chief. Clyde took the vacant seat in the pew behind them.

A few other members of the hospital staff were also present, two young student nurses, a staff nurse and theater nurse. Clyde wondered whether they were surprised to see the superintendent sitting with Matron. And if he was embarrassed to be seen in church with Ruth, Dr. Ashmore didn't show it. He sat listening to the service with his natural detachment, his gray eyes fixed straight ahead of him. He hardly seemed aware of the woman at his side.

Joyfully Clyde joined in the singing of the familiar hymn,

> Praise, my soul, the King of heaven;
> To His feet thy tribute bring;
> Ransomed, healed, restored, forgiven,
> Who like thee His praise should sing?
> Praise Him, praise Him,
> Praise the everlasting King.

The minister spoke on the power of influence that each person, consciously or unconsciously, wielded over another. The message could not have been more appropriate than if it had been especially prepared for the case of Dr. Ashmore and Penny Fielding. ". . . Hear the words of our Lord in Matthew 18:6: 'Whoso shall offend one of these little ones which believe in me, it were better for him that a millstone were hanged about his neck, and that he were drowned in the depths of the sea.' These are very grave and stern words. To destroy deliberately another's faith in God deserves the greatest punishment . . . ."

Clyde, keenly observing his chief's reaction, saw the dull flush which spread over his face and neck. It was the first time that the intern could recall ever seeing his superior display embarrassment of any kind. The preaching of the Gospel obviously affected him deeply.

CHAPTER NINE

After the service Clyde did not expect to find Penny waiting for him. She had stood behind a large tree and had watched surreptitiously as the congregation had filed out of church. She just had to make sure that Michael Ashmore had actually been present at the service.

It was incredible that he who prided himself on being an agnostic, he who had scoffingly declared many times that church-going was nothing but hypocrisy, should now suddenly want to attend a church service. There must be a reason for such a change of attitude, Penny decided, and the reason was none other than Ruth van Rhyn.

Penny had seen Matron come down the steps of the church with the medical superintendent gallantly holding her arm.

So it was true! Penny suppressed a little shiver. There was the glow of rapture on Ruth's face. She could not say how Michael looked — his face had suddenly become a blur.

Almost fiercely Penny dabbed her eyes. It was utterly ridiculous for her to feel this way just because Michael had decided to accompany Matron to church. Perhaps he had only consented to attend the service out of his deep respect for her. There was probably nothing more to it than that.

She took a firm grip on herself and approached the intern.

"Penny! It's good of you to call for me, but I could quite easily have walked, you know. Where did you park?"

As Clyde walked beside her, he became aware that something was troubling the girl. She was shaking slightly.

"What's the matter, Penny?" he asked with concern.

Her lips quivered. "I saw them — Doctor and Matron. I came along to see for myself. I just had to be certain — not that I didn't believe you — you might have been mistaken. But you were absolutely right. He was in church with Ruth! Oh, Michael — Michael — !" Penny began to sob brokenly.

Solicitously Clyde took her arm and helped her into the car.

Taking the ignition key from her, he said: "I'll drive. Now you sit here quietly till we get back, then we can talk."

There was reassurance in his calm tone. By the time they had reached the house, Penny had herself under some control.

"I'm sorry, Clyde. I'm being a fool, I know. Let's go into Father's old study — I've turned it into a little sitting room. It's cozier than the lounge."

The room perfectly reflected Penny's warm, bright personality. No longer did the room look cold and austere. It was gaily decorated. The colorful curtains blended excellently with the wall-to-wall carpet. The antique, canebacked chairs had been replaced by a suite of modern design. The evidence of wealth was everywhere.

"I'll ring for some tea. I'm thirsty." Penny pressed a bell. "You'll have tea, Clyde?"

He nodded. "Thanks. But I ought not to stay too long."

"You're off somewhere else? A girl friend, perhaps?"

He laughed. "No fear! I'm off to bed. I like my sleep. I've spent a long, tiring day in Casualty. I want to be fresh for my work tomorrow morning."

There was a discreet knock on the door. In response to Penny's "Come in!" a servant entered with a tray.

Penny walked over to the record player. "Would you like me to put on a record for you while we have tea?" she asked, turning to Clyde.

She saw his hesitation. "It will be a most conventional record, I assure you." She flashed him one of her lovely smiles. "I had enough of pop music when I was out with Don Anderson last night."

So Penny was still going out with the E.N.T. surgeon. But why her strange reaction on learning that the Medical Superintendent had attended church with Matron? Clyde didn't think Penny was the type of girl who would encourage a man while caring for another.

She continued: "We came back only at two o'clock this morning — or was it three? I was so sleepy that I slept right through until lunch time today. Fancy sleeping so late on a Sunday morning! I should have been on the beach enjoying the lovely

58

weather." She paused, her eyes dancing with merriment. "What a sinner you must think me. I daresay in your opinion everyone who doesn't go to church is considered a dreadful sinner."

Gladly Clyde took up the challenge. "We are all sinners, Penny, whether we attend church or not. The Word of God declares that 'all have sinned and come short of the glory of God.' We are all in need of cleansing and forgiveness."

"But I don't believe in God," she pertly reminded the intern. "Besides, I haven't done anything really wicked, you know. You can't possibly place me in the same category as a murderer — or a thief, for instance. I'm not really bad," she pouted petulantly.

He smiled tolerantly. "All the same, in God's sight you are classed as a sinner. Even I am a sinner — "

"You!" she ejaculated, almost dropping a record in her astonishment. "Why, what wrong have you done, Clyde?"

He grinned. "Nothing spectacular, I assure you. The same as you, I've led an ordinary, decent life. But one day the Lord convicted me that I was a sinner who needed His pardon. His Word says: 'If we confess our sins He is faithful and just to forgive us our sins and to cleanse us from all unrighteousness.' Gratefully I accepted His forgiveness and committed my life to God. Now I have a wonderful Saviour."

"But I don't believe in God," she reiterated, knitting her brows in puzzlement. She placed the record back in the stand and began to pour the tea. She handed Clyde a cup. "At least I don't think I believe in God."

"Don't you, Penny?" he probed gently. "I suspect you haven't given the matter serious consideration. Most people don't until they're faced with an illness, or are admitted into hospital as an accident case. You haven't really thought about God at all."

"You're right, I haven't," she admitted with a rueful shake of her head. "Thinking about God makes me morbid. It's not a pleasant subject, really. I've always been taught that it's not good manners to discuss religion. So if you don't mind, Clyde — " she gestured eloquently.

"Very well — if that's how you feel. But first tell me this. Have you ever given a thought to the marvels of nature? We see the evidence of God's handiwork all around us. 'The heavens declare the glory of God and the firmament showeth his handiwork.' That's a quotation from Psalm 19:1. Trees, flowers, birds, the stately mountains, hills and valleys, the restless ocean — all these tell of His glory." Clyde spoke with great enthusiasm. "Have you ever stopped to watch a beautiful sunset or a sunrise?"

Penny nodded. She was looking at the doctor with new eyes. Behind his quiet, pleasant exterior there was unsuspected force of character.

Reflectively she sipped her tea. "I have frequently paused to admire a splendid sunset. Its beauty has not failed to move me yet."

"Then how can you possibly say there is no God?" He thrust out his chin in a gesture that was to become familiar to her. "Let's think of the moon for a moment. If the moon were not just at its exact distance from the earth, the ocean tides would inundate the land mass completely twice a day. If the ocean were just a few feet deeper, the carbon dioxide and oxygen in the earth's atmosphere would be completely absorbed and no vegetable life could exist on earth. Scientists have discovered these facts to be absolutely true. Don't you see, Penny?" Clyde pleaded earnestly. The light in his eyes burned brightly. "This wonderful, scientifically designed earth did not just happen; there's not a chance in a million for that. Science proves beyond all doubt that God did design and create the universe."

She stifled a yawn. "I'm afraid I'm not exactly up on these matters," she confessed with an uncertain smile. "At school science wasn't my favorite subject. Dad wanted me to go to the university, but as I wasn't at all keen on the idea, he allowed me to attend secretarial college instead. Like you, Michael attended the university. He must have studied the subject, yet he maintains we can't be sure there is a God."

"Dr. Ashmore may have studied, but let me assure you he did not study these subjects in relation to God's Word, otherwise it would have been revealed to him that scientifically and historically the Bible is absolutely true." Clyde smiled. "In all ways, the Bible is true — "

Penny checked his words with a gesture of annoyance.

"Michael Ashmore is a clever man. I'd rather go by what he says. He must have studied these matters for himself to form his own conclusions."

"But what if the chief should change his views?"

"You mean to say he may change his views just because he went to church with Ruth?" Penny did not seem pleased at the idea.

"Not necessarily. Church attendance does not make one a

60

Christian, you know. It is a personal faith in God — one must believe that Christ died and rose again from the dead. We must accept the Lord as our own Saviour, believe that He suffered for our sins on the Cross."

Penny put down her cup. "I should hardly think Doctor would swallow such nonsense. He's not a sinner! He's a good, decent man — and I should know! But even if he did become a believer, it would make no difference to me. I'd say he was being influenced by Ruth. It's my opinion Matron is after Doctor herself. And should he become a Christian, I'd blame Ruth. Yes, I would." Penny clenched her small hands. "She has no right to try to influence him — why can't she leave him alone?" Her voice rose in anger.

Clyde was silent. He was unprepared for such a tempestuous reaction.

"I mean it," Penny went on with an emphatic nod of her head. "I'd blame Ruth if Michael decided to embrace the Christian faith. But he needn't think I'd ever entertain the idea of becoming a believer. I'm quite satisfied as I am, thank you!"

Still Clyde did not speak. Penny was not the docile little girl he had at first imagined. She was the late Henry Fielding's daughter. Undoubtedly she had inherited the great man's determination — a determination that at times could amount to sheer obstinacy.

He emerged from his thoughts as Penny spoke.

"What would happen to me if Michael should become a believer, or if he should become attached to Ruth? Doctor is my whole life. I have no one but him."

"Have you no relatives — no one to whom you can turn?"

She shook her head a little sadly. "No one at all. I believe I have a few distant relatives still living over in England. But I haven't seen them for years. We didn't keep in touch. My mother died before we came out to South Africa. And that was years ago. I was only a small girl."

"I'm sorry. I'd no idea you were so alone. But — forgive my mentioning this — the hospital grapevine has it that you're friendly with the E.N.T. surgeon. Surely if that's the case and you decide to marry him — "

With a laugh, Penny cut in: "Marry Don Anderson! Not I! Now don't misunderstand me. Don is quite a nice fellow — we've had some grand times together. But it's Michael I love — there will never be anyone for me but Michael. Oh, I know what you're going to say — he's too old for me. But I like an older man — I must have someone I can lean upon, someone I can trust. Michael is necessary to me — I'd be quite lost without him."

"I don't think that at all. You would find your feet all right. You would then learn to think for yourself instead of accepting blindly another's point of view. Besides, I do consider the chief is too old for you." The intern hesitated.

"Go on," Penny commanded. "I do want to know what else you may have to say."

"Perhaps not if there was true love on either side." Clyde paused again.

"Go on."

"Please don't take offense at what I have to say. In my opinion, you and Dr. Ashmore are not temperamentally suited."

"Just what do you mean by that? I promise not to take offense," she said as she observed Clyde's reluctance to continue.

"You are essentially warmhearted. Dr. Ashmore's reserve, his unresponsiveness may eventually hurt you. Maybe there is hidden warmth underneath his coldness — only the woman he loved and who loved him in return would discover that, and should you marry Doctor for any other reason than love, you might sadly regret it one day."

"But I do love him!" she protested. "As I've already said there will never be another man but Michael. I have no intention of marrying anyone else."

"If that's the case, what on earth do you mean by going out with Don Anderson?" Clyde questioned in a stern tone she had not heard before.

"Just what are you implying?"

"What I've said. How can you even consider going out with another man when it's Dr. Ashmore you love?"

Penny chuckled suddenly. "I thought it a good idea to make Michael sit up and take notice. I thought it would do him a world of good if I went out with someone else. Don adores me — he has even proposed to me. Of course I wouldn't dream of accepting him. But I do enjoy his attentions and I intend to continue to go out with him."

"But that's hardly playing the game. It's not being fair, Penny."

A flush mounted her cheeks. "I wanted to make Michael jealous."

Inexorably Clyde went on: "How could you encourage Anderson to propose to you when you have not the slightest intention of marrying the man? And how can you continue to use him as an escort when your motive is all wrong?"

She jumped to her feet, her eyes sparkling with indignation.

"How dare you take it upon yourself to act as my judge? You're nothing but a self-righteous prig, Clyde Maxwell! I'm sorry I asked you to come here tonight."

He rose to his feet. "Sorry to have offended you." The grave way in which he spoke gave his pleasant face a new dignity. "Goodnight, Penny." Resolutely he strode to the door.

Immediately she came and placed a hand on his arm. "I'm sorry, Clyde. That was nasty of me. Am I forgiven?"

"Of course." There was a new restraint about him.

"Then come and sit down again."

"I must really be going."

"Oh, dear! So I am not completely forgiven." There was a note of accusation in her voice.

Clyde sat down. He was aware of sharp disappointment, whether at his own behavior or Penny's, he could not tell.

His manner to her was more formal. It worried her. What on earth must he be thinking of her? Clyde's words were quite true, she realized with an awakening pang of conscience. She had no right to enjoy Don's attention, his flattery, when she clearly had no other motive than to make Michael jealous. But the galling part was this — that instead of having the desired effect upon Dr. Ashmore, his chief reaction had been to warn her of Don's hot temper. That was the only reason why he had urged her to tread carefully where the E.N.T. surgeon was concerned.

"Sorry to have sounded so pompous." Clyde smiled suddenly across at her.

"I feel so ashamed, Clyde." Penny raised a pair of appealing blue eyes to his. "I know now I have made a mistake — I certainly should not have encouraged Don — or given him any cause of hope. But I was lonely — and Don made an attractive escort. He can be stimulating company, you know. Many of the nurses are keen on him, especially Staff Nurse Gregory. She must be feeling pretty much the same as I'm feeling as regards Michael going out with Ruth. Poor Phyl Gregory! No wonder she ignores me. I can't get a smile out of her."

"I don't know anything about Staff Nurse Gregory," Clyde rejoined, "but I do know that you have nothing to fear in regard to Matron's relationship with the chief. Ruth is trying to help him spiritually, that is all."

"But how can you be so certain?" Penny queried anxiously.

Clyde smiled reassuringly. "I know Ruth. So please don't bother your head any more about the matter, Penny."

She breathed a sigh of relief and flashed him a smile.

"I shall accept your word, Clyde. I only hope that you're not mistaken."

CHAPTER TEN

The following morning when Penny entered the medical superintendent's office, she noted immediately the bowl of exquisite peace roses on his desk.

Penny's first reaction was one of annoyance. Then she reasoned with herself. She had no right really to feel resentful. For years now Ruth had taken it upon herself to see that there were always fresh flowers in Dr. Ashmore's office.

Some months back Ruth had observed Penny wistfully watching her arrange the flowers. So she had kindly suggested that the younger girl do them occasionally. "But mind you tell me the days when you intend to do so," Ruth had added, "otherwise we'll both be bringing flowers on the same day."

This Penny would invariably fail to do. She brought flowers to the hospital whenever the mood took her. Frequently Ruth would have to remove her blooms to one of the wards. This she did without a murmur, without even a reproachful look at the younger girl. Sometimes her disappointment was reflected in her expressive eyes.

Leaning over the roses, Penny inhaled their delicate fragrance. *They're lovely*, she mused. What was it that Clyde had said? "Have you ever given a thought to the marvels of nature? We see the evidence of God's handiwork all around us." The words he had quoted from Psalms, "The heavens declare the glory of God and the firmament showeth his handiwork," came back to her with startling clarity.

Last night she had not slept well, an unusual occurrence for her. Confused thoughts had chased themselves around her mind. She had been disturbed far more than she had admitted to Clyde by the fact of Michael's attendance at church with Ruth.

Dr. Ashmore was Penny's whole world — her very existence. Since her father's death, she had come to rely upon him in almost everything. Her emotional nature demanded an outlet — someone on whom she could lavish her boundless affection.

The worship and love she should have given to God — which was His by sovereign right — she had blindly, illogically poured out on Dr. Ashmore.

Her mind torn by conflicting emotions, she went into her own office. The sound of voices reached her ears as the next moment the door to the medical superintendent's office opened. Michael's voice blended with that of Ruth van Rhyn.

He was remarking: "I can't say I really enjoyed the service. I found it interesting, though. There was plenty of food for thought in what the preacher said. In fact, part of the sermon kept me awake last night."

"I'm sorry . . . ." Penny heard Matron murmur. But she didn't sound very convincing.

"Does that mean you wouldn't care to come again?" Ruth inquired, much to Penny's annoyance.

"Not at all — not at all. I'd like to come again. Very much, in fact," he added after a long pause.

Penny held her breath as Dr. Ashmore asked: "What about next Sunday?"

She could imagine Ruth's smile of pure delight.

"It's my day off on Sunday. I'm back on duty at five o'clock, so I won't be able to attend the evening service but I am free to go Sunday morning."

"Splendid!" Dr. Ashmore sounded pleased. "That will suit me fine. Strange, but now I want to be present at the service for my own sake. It's suddenly become most important to me that I discover the truth for myself." There was a small pause. Then: "Perhaps you would care to have lunch with me afterwards at my club?"

This was too much for Penny. She felt faint and giddy. Her little world of dreams came tottering to the ground.

Clyde was mistaken! This was no mere friendship. It was more like the beginning of a courtship — Michael's and Ruth's.

The thought shattered Penny completely. She had to hold on to her desk to steady herself. All color drained from her face.

For a few moments she was unable to move. Then, resolutely gathering her strength, she walked slowly into the superintendent's office.

"Hullo, Penny!" Michael's voice joined Ruth's to greet her pleasantly.

"Oh, hullo." Without success she tried to instill some enthusiasm into her voice. She shot Ruth a look bordering on hostility. Matron's observant eyes noted the girl's pallor.

"Penny, my dear, is anything the matter?" There was concern in the question.

"Why, no — " her voice trailed off lamely.

"Look, Penny, would you mind coming into my office for a minute? There's something I'd like to say to you. Please excuse us, Doctor." Firmly Ruth held on to Penny's arm.

Matron closed the door to her office and seated the trembling girl in a chair.

Ruth looked searchingly into Penny's face. "Now tell me what's troubling you."

"I — " Penny moistened her dry lips. "Who said anything about trouble? I'm not feeling well, that's all there is to it." She rose in her chair.

"Sit down," Matron commanded in the authoritative voice she employed to her nursing staff. "We must clear this matter up if we're to continue to work harmoniously together."

Penny's head went up aggressively. "I'm in no way responsible to you. Dr. Ashmore is my employer, and I am answerable to him alone. I think you've taken too much upon yourself, Miss van Rhyn."

Matron smiled. "Perhaps I have." She was undecided for a moment. Then she remarked: "I'm afraid you appear to be laboring under some kind of misapprehension."

"In which way?" Penny's lips quivered.

Again Ruth was undecided. She was under no obligation to explain her friendship with Dr. Ashmore to Penny. It was entirely her own affair. But for the sake of the girl's peace of mind, she decided it would be best to be frank with her.

Ruth placed a gentle hand on Penny's shoulder.

"Oh, Ruth, I'm so miserable!" she burst out, too desperate any longer to pretend. "So utterly and completely miserable. Why did you have to take Doctor away from me? Why!" Angry, baffled tears welled up in her blue eyes.

Matron said quietly: "I've not taken Dr. Ashmore away from you. The chief belongs to neither of us."

"That's what you would say," Penny spoke wretchedly. "Doctor belongs to me. He is all I have to hold on to. He is my only anchor in life. I'd be utterly lost without him." She wrung her hands in a gesture of despair.

Vague presentiments clutched at Ruth's heart. When she spoke she was amazed at the steadiness of her voice.

"I am well aware, of course, of your deep attachment to Dr. Ashmore. But I'd no idea you felt quite so strongly about him. You love him very much?"

"I do!" There was defiance in Penny's voice. "I love him desperately. So there!"

Matron knew a sense of inadequacy. Before making reply, she breathed a prayer for guidance in dealing with an awkward situation.

"Now you know why I'm so worried," Penny resumed. "It would mean the end for me if you should take Doctor away from me."

"But my dear girl," protested Ruth, "I have no such thoughts in my head. Sorry if I have given you a false impression."

With vigor, Penny demanded: "Then what is your motive in inviting Doctor to church? I saw you together last night."

Matron smiled slowly. "I see . . . . Would you like to know the reason why Dr. Ashmore decided to attend the service last night?"

"Please . . . . " Penny lowered her eyes before the other's level gaze.

"It was for your sake, Penny."

"For my sake?" she echoed incredulously.

"Yes. Now you know what prompted me to ask you here into my office. I wanted to explain to you. I guessed you must have heard that Doctor and I have been seen together recently. That's why you were so upset. Please let me put your mind at rest, Penny. There is nothing — absolutely nothing between the chief and me. Lately he's become disturbed because you have accepted his agnostic views. I loaned him a book that set him thinking. Next he asked if he might take me to church. That's all there is to it."

"Oh, dear!" A feeling of shame stole over Penny. "I'm sorry, Ruth. I seem to have jumped to absurd conclusions. Please forgive me."

"Of course." Ruth smiled generously. "Perhaps you would care to accompany Doctor and me to church next Sunday morning?"

Penny stiffened. "I'd rather not, thanks. Even if Michael should be persuaded to become a Christian, it would make no difference to me. I'm just not interested in churchgoing."

"I thought you said you loved Dr. Ashmore," Ruth reminded the younger girl.

"I do. I do! I've loved him for four years now."

Ruth heaved an inward sigh. *And I have loved him for fourteen long years . . . .*

With a start she emerged from her reverie. Penny was asking: "I know I'm being a nuisance, but are you positive there isn't anything between you and Michael?"

Ruth's first impulse was to tell the younger girl to mind her own business. But seeing the anxiety in the blue eyes, she rejoined firmly: "Absolutely positive. So please put that absurd idea right out of your mind."

Penny sighed loudly. "I suppose I'm being silly. But I have a sort of premonition — a foreboding. I can't seem to shake it off." She paused, passing a perplexing hand across her brow. "You say Doctor came to church with you for my sake. But what about Thursday evening? You were seen entering a restaurant together."

Ruth did not speak. Penny continued: "Please forgive me for being so inquisitive. But I must know."

Reflectively Ruth drummed her fingers on her desk. "That is correct. Doctor asked me out to discuss a book with me."

Penny pulled a wry face. "Not since Father's death has Michael taken me out anywhere." She spoke resentfully. "Yet he takes you out to discuss a book. What exactly is his purpose?"

Ruth was beginning to feel slightly jaded. But she rejoined patiently: "Again Doctor was worried about you. He agreed to read the book solely in order to help you. The book fascinated him — he became absorbed in it and wanted to discuss certain aspects with me. Now please, Penny, I can't afford to waste any more time over this business. Why don't you ask Dr. Ashmore yourself?"

Penny said hastily: "Oh, no, I couldn't do that! He might take offense and tell me to mind my own business. At times he can be most caustic, as you perhaps may know."

"You don't seem very sure of him," Matron murmered.

Again Penny sighed. "I'm not. I haven't a clue as to his real feelings for me."

"I know he feels a certain responsibility toward you."

Penny shrugged. "Could be. But that's only because of his

friendship with Father. So now Doctor is concerned because I have adopted his agnostic views. He thinks that by attending church he can become a Christian and I will automatically become one, too. How nice!"

The note of scorn in Penny's voice worried Ruth.

"You're mistaken, Penny. Dr. Ashmore knows by now that attending God's house does not make one a Christian. And it's a mistake for anyone to rely on church affiliation to get them into heaven. My church membership did not make me a child of God. It was my personal belief in the Living God, my acceptance of Him as my Saviour."

Penny looked a little bemused. "That's what Clyde said last night. He seems to share your views. And now you are doing your level best to influence Doctor to accept them as well."

Ruth smiled. "Not my views. The Word of God declares that these facts are true. Read the Bible and then you will see for yourself, Penny. At present Doctor is doing just that. He is studying science in relation to God's Word. And he is simply astounded at what he has discovered and is discovering daily. It shouldn't be long now before he finds out the truth for himself."

"That should make you extremely happy."

Ruth ignored the sarcasm in the younger girl's voice. "Naturally. I'm always glad when someone who has walked in darkness one day sees the light. When a soul turns to the Lord Jesus and commits his life to Him, it is the most wonderful and glorious thing that could happen to anyone. It is an experience worth having. Try it and see for yourself, Penny."

She set her lips in an obstinate line. "I should hate it if Michael became a Christian. It would be the end for me. Life wouldn't be worth living." The utter desolation in her voice shocked Ruth.

"But why, Penny?"

"Why?" The blue eyes filled with anguish. "You know full well the answer to that one! Michael is all I have in life. If he should become a believer, he would naturally turn to you. He is doing that already. Oh, don't you see, Ruth — !" Penny's voice was raised in distress. "I couldn't bear to lose Michael to you — or to anyone else. He is the only one who matters to me. Without him life would be meaningless. And if he should marry you — "

"Nonsense!" Matron remonstrated with some force. "Dr. Ashmore has no romantic interest in me whatsoever. Now let's hear no more of this sort of talk. I shall continue to pray that Doctor will become a Christian and that you too, Penny, will see the light." Ruth stood up.

"By the way, I was going to ask a favor of you, Penny. It's about Robin. Have you any spare time to read to him? Clyde would be most grateful to you."

Penny nodded, some of the unhappiness leaving her eyes. "Clyde spoke to me about that last night. I promised I would."

"Good." Ruth wondered where Penny had met Clyde. But she did not voice her question.

"Now, my dear, you'd better get back to Doctor's office or we'll have him ringing for you."

After Penny left her, Ruth sat for a long while lost in thought. The young girl was going to prove a problem, a most difficult problem indeed.

CHAPTER ELEVEN

Penny decided to work right through her lunch hour so that she would be free part of the afternoon to read to Robin.

After the superintendent's customary morning conference with his staff, when the case book and various reports were discussed, Dr. Ashmore had dictated practically the rest of the morning. He had been preoccupied and aloof and had scarcely noticed her presence. Penny felt hurt and bewildered.

It's Ruth, Penny concluded, her resentment of Matron flaring up again. She had observed them talking together after the doctors had left the Superintendent's office. On Michael's face was a look of animation which she had not seen previously. Ruth's expressive eyes were unusually guarded, as if she had been afraid they might reveal too much.

I've been extremely foolish, Penny chided herself, *to let Ruth see just how much I care for Michael . . . .*

With the determination she had inherited from her late father, she finished the letters in record time.

Dr. Ashmore glanced up absently as she placed them on his desk for his signature.

"Finished already? Good girl." Then with a gesture of dismissal, he inclined his head to study some papers on his desk.

She thought: *I simply don't exist for him . . . .* She bit her lip hard.

Smiling tremulously, she gazed down at his bent head, at the small bald patch which until now she had not noticed. She hadn't thought of Michael as ever growing old. To her he had always seemed ageless. Michael was hers forever. She would not allow Ruth van Rhyn to take him away from her.

I'll stop her somehow! Penny vowed.

72

As if suddenly becoming aware of her presence, Dr. Ashmore glanced up. A cool smile played upon his lips.

"What, still here! Thought you had planned to read to the Radford boy. Most likely you'll find Robin out on the balcony sunning himself. Now run along, there's a good girl. Have a pleasant time."

Penny fumbled nervously with the buttons of her jacket. Why did Michael persist in treating her as if she were still a child? Tears of mortification stung her eyes.

"Michael — " Desperately Penny plunged on. "Forgive my asking. Is there anything between you and Ruth van Rhyn?"

"I beg your pardon!" His fine brows rose in displeasure. "Please explain yourself, Penny." He swung round in his revolving chair.

"I'm sorry," she faltered, blushing furiously. "I'm not just being inquisitive."

"You are!" he interposed in a cold, stern voice which caused her to regret voicing her question. "And impertinent as well!" He raised a long, elegant hand. "Now let's hear no more of this sort of talk."

"I'm sorry," she repeated, her blue eyes full of unshed tears. How remote, how unsympathetic he appeared. Her whole being cried out for kindness, for affection. "I didn't mean to offend you — truly I didn't. It's just that — " she broke off in confusion.

She sounded so crestfallen, so utterly dejected that the doctor permitted a tolerant smile to touch his lips.

"What's the trouble, my girl? You've been looking somewhat peakish today. Young Anderson giving you a spot of bother?"

Did she detect sympathetic concern in Michael's voice?

"Why, no — " Don Anderson had not been in her thoughts all day.

Dr. Ashmore appeared to be pondering deeply. Then he remarked: "Penny, I have something to say to you. Please sit down while I tell you. I am no longer an agnostic. Maybe you will be relieved to know that now I am absolutely and completely convinced that there is a God."

Penny hoped fervently that her face registered none of the shock she felt. Under different circumstances she would doubtless have been pleased to hear the news. After Clyde's discussion with her last night, she herself was beginning to think that perhaps after all God did exist. But now, poignantly aware of Michael's friendship with Matron, Penny's chief feeling was one of disaster. The fact that he now believed in the existence of God would undoubtedly bring him and Ruth closer together.

The thought struck a chill in Penny's heart. This latest development could well threaten her future happiness with Michael.

In a strange voice she heard herself ask: "How can you be sure there is a Supreme Being?"

He pursed his lips in a contemplative line. "It's somewhat difficult to explain. For many years I have doubted the existence of God. But now, in my own mind, I have complete assurance that God is alive. Everything in nature, in history, in physical and medical science points to the indisputable fact that He does exist, that the Bible is His Word and that He is indeed the Creator of the universe. How blind I have been these long years! I refused to read a book dealing with these matters; I refused even to consider the idea that maybe I was wrong."

Dr. Ashmore paused. His gray eyes were meditative.

"One thing bothers me, though. I now have a little head knowledge of Him without a heart knowledge. But Matron is quite confident that in good time everything will be revealed to me."

Penny was stung into replying: "I wouldn't go by what Ruth van Rhyn thinks or says. She could be so wrong, you know."

He shook his head firmly. "You are completely mistaken, Penny. I have not been influenced by Matron's opinion of these things. I have formed my own conclusions. I have studied the Bible — "

"That's what Ruth said," Penny broke in, looking slightly dazed. "I just can't believe it! It doesn't seem possible. You used to be such a skeptic, Michael. If I remember correctly, nothing whatsoever would induce you to read the Bible, much less glance at it. A book of fables and myths, you would frequently declare." She frowned. "Matron must have influenced you very strongly. What on earth induced you to become interested in religion all of a sudden?"

Here was Dr. Ashmore's opportunity. "I was concerned about you, my girl."

"That's what Ruth said," Penny muttered, "and I wouldn't believe her . . . . "

The medical superintendent pursued: "When I learned that you had adopted my agnostic views, I was most disturbed, and I determined at once to do something about the matter. But in order to discuss things more fully with you, I had to study for myself. I must confess that the idea of studying these subjects had not occurred to me until recently."

Penny made no comment. She was thinking: *So Ruth was speaking the truth. All the same, I don't like it — I don't like it one bit. I wish Michael would give up the idea of studying religion.*

Dr. Ashmore was saying: "Matron has kindly agreed to give me a few Bible lessons."

Oh, no! Appalled, Penny checked the words that tumbled to her lips. This would surely mean the end of her cherished hopes, her dreams.

A soft knock sounded on the door. Then Matron entered the office, looking so serene, so assured that Penny felt gauche and immature by contrast.

How could she ever hope to compete against such poise, such composure, Penny asked herself wretchedly.

Dr. Ashmore and Matron smiled genially at each other. To add to Penny's distress, some sort of secret signal seemed to pass between them.

As if suddenly becoming aware of Penny, a guarded look leaped into Ruth's eyes. "Hope I'm not intruding," she began tentatively.

"Penny is just on the point of leaving," Dr. Ashmore remarked, much to her chagrin. "She has promised to read to Robin Radford."

She had no option but to rise to her feet. Smiling, Ruth sat down in the chair Penny had just vacated.

"Enjoy yourself," said Matron pleasantly.

Penny gave a helpless shrug and rushed out of the office.

She encountered Clyde in the main corridor.

"Hullo! How are you today?" he inquired cordially. He flashed her a keen glance and, with a physician's perception, saw that she was still in a somewhat agitated frame of mind. She appeared strained and tense, unlike her usual happy, carefree self.

"Oh, I'm fine thanks." Penny endeavored a smile. She was plucking nervously at her jacket. "I've had a busy morning, but now I'm free to read to Robin."

The intern's face lit up. "Splendid! Robin will be delighted. You'll find him on the balcony that leads off the boys' ward. I'm on my way to see the chief but I'll be with you directly. Till then."

Her confidence somewhat restored by Clyde's cheerful manner, Penny walked through the long ward and came face to face with Staff Nurse Gregory, who flung the younger girl a look of pure contempt.

This time the other's attitude stung Penny. She couldn't really blame Phyl for her animosity. Doubtless she was of the opinion that Penny was doing her utmost to capture Don Anderson and had now succeeded. The staff nurse was not to know that Penny had merely been amusing herself with him and had endeavored to use him for her own ends.

No wonder Clyde had seemed so shocked. She could now well understand his vigorous reaction.

Unexpectedly, a sense of shame stole over her. Then a horrifying thought struck her. Perhaps she, too, was a sinner! Last night Clyde had pointed out to her from God's Word that all were sinners — all had come short of the glory of God.

But I don't believe in God, Penny reminded herself forcibly. *At least I don't think I do.* Unconsciously she put a confused hand to her forehead.

She found Robin reclining in one of the canvas chairs. The sun shone on his tousled head; his blue eyes were alight with mischief as he peered up at Penny.

"Hullo, Robin! Enjoying the sunshine?" She drew a chair next to his and seated herself. "My, it's warm in the sun. At this rate you'll be getting a few more freckles on your nose." His face was already powdered with freckles.

The boy grinned. "That won't matter. I'm not a sissy."

"Of course you're not! You're fast growing into a strong man. I see you have a book there."

He nodded and with a grimace turned the book over to show her the title. "Uncle Clyde gave it to me this morning. I haven't looked at it yet. I'm not too keen on Bible stories. I want to be a tough guy. I prefer to read about cowboys and spacemen." He paused. "Don't you?"

"Well — " She tried to infuse some interest into her voice. "Perhaps. But Bible stories can be exciting as well. I remember hearing the story of the Prodigal Son when I was a young girl. I found it most fascinating. Here, let me see if I can find it for you in this book. Yes, here we are. Would you like me to read it?"

He pulled a wry face. "I suppose it will be all right," he agreed without enthusiasm.

As Penny read the story of the Prodigal Son, her mind slipped back down the corridor of time. She was again a young teen-ager, sitting demurely in church next to Ruth van Rhyn, her hands clasped as in rapt attention she listened to the preacher telling of the love of God. She had then believed in God, had been hungry to hear more about that wonderful love; she had earnestly joined the many others in the singing of "There is no love like the love of Jesus . . . ."

Then had followed her discussion with Dr. Ashmore, who had scoffed at her childish beliefs. Michael had destroyed — unwittingly perhaps — her faith in God. But now he had found God — at least, he was well on the way to discovering Him.

Now, illogically, Penny dreaded the dawning of that day, dreaded the time when she would hear him say — "Well, Penny, at last I have found the Lord. I believe that He died for my sins and I have now committed my life into His keeping."

It would mean the end, the complete finish where she was concerned. When Michael — there could be no ifs now — became a Christian, he would naturally turn to Ruth for fellowship; their friendship would be more firmly cemented. The thought was frightening. Involuntarily Penny shuddered.

Michael — oh, Michael! her heart cried in anguish.

"Do you believe in God, Miss Fielding?" Robin's voice broke into her ruminations.

Gallantly Penny choked back the sobs in her throat. She could not possibly destroy this child's faith in God, no matter how much she personally doubted His existence. She could not be as callous, as unthinking, as Michael had been that Sunday five years ago.

She said: "Of course I do!" She was successful in putting some conviction into her voice.

"You do?" Thoughtfully the boy brushed a lock of red hair from his forehead. "So does Uncle Clyde. He told me that God sent His Son to die for our sins, because He loves us so much."

Penny nodded. "That's quite correct. God does love you, Robin."

"Even if I have done something dreadful?" Suddenly his lips were quivering.

"I guess so." Penny was out of her depths. She wished fervently that Clyde would soon put in an appearance.

Common sense came to her rescue. "Let's see what it says here in this story. After his wanderings in sin and shame, the Prodigal

77

Son said: 'I will arise and return to my father and will say to him; Father, I have sinned against your God and against you and am no more worthy to be called your son; make me one of your hired servants. And he arose and returned to his father. But when he was still a long way off, his father saw him and was moved with pity and tenderness and ran and put his arms round his neck and kissed him — ' "

"Oh!" Into Robin's face came a dawning wonder. "That means his father was prepared to take him back even though he had sinned."

"Yes. That's it, I guess." Again Penny was out of her depths.

"Then — then — " he was stammering almost incoherently, "there is hope for me."

"Of course there is," she assured him, but she felt far from assured herself. "Why, what have you done, Robin?"

She perceived that he was bravely fighting tears.

"I — I — It wasn't quite an accident, Miss Fielding. Hitting my ear was — the other wasn't. Deliberately I took out the pistol intending to — "

"What wasn't?" she mumbled absently. Then, as his words penetrated, she gasped: "Oh, Robin! You don't mean — you can't mean — !" Aghast, she stared at the boy.

He was sobbing now. Subdued sobs shook his shoulders.

"I — I intended to harm her. I wanted to hurt her! Not kill her — just to hurt her, you understand. She wouldn't let me do anything that I wanted. My mother always let me do things — she didn't object — "

"Oh, dear." Penny drew a long, hard breath. Hopefully she looked up. With a throb of thankfulness she saw Clyde striding towards them.

He glanced questioningly at the distraught boy, then at Penny.

"What's the trouble?" he asked briefly.

"Robin has just confessed that he intended to harm your sister."

The intern was silent. His pleasant face was unusually grave.

"I've suspected that," he admitted. "These last few days the idea has come to me." He placed his hand compassionately on the boy's shoulder while Robin cried out his grief. Curious eyes were upon them, but Clyde carried on as if he and the boy were shut in a private room.

Scarcely daring to move, Penny silently watched the scene.

"Robin, my boy, there's no need for you to cry any more. If you are truly sorry for what you have done, God will readily forgive you. He is just waiting and longing for you to come to Him. He wants you to trust Him. Remember the Bible tells us God is love."

"I — " the boy gulped, wiping his eyes furiously. "It was that part in the story where the son returned to his father and his father put his arms round him and kissed him that made me want to cry. Daddy doesn't love me any more — he just loves your sister now. He has no time for me now; he'd never forgive me for what I've done. Please don't tell him, Uncle Clyde."

"But if you want the Lord to forgive you, you must confess your sins," the doctor reminded Robin, his hand still on the boy's shoulder.

"Oh, I will confess to God," the boy promised, his face brightening. "I know He will forgive me. The Bible tells me so. But my daddy doesn't love me." Tears gathered once more in the boy's eyes.

"Of course he does! Your father has done everything he can to show you his love. He comes to see you every day. He has given up important engagements just to be near you. That surely proves how much he loves you."

"I feel so guilty," Robin said in a muffled voice. His eyes were filled with remorse. "Do you think you can pray for me, Uncle Clyde?"

The intern knew it was the Holy Spirit who had convicted Robin of his sin and of his need of the Saviour.

Reverently Clyde lifted his heart to the Lord in prayer. He pleaded earnestly that Robin would put his trust in the Lord Jesus who had died upon the Cross for his sins. His simple prayer touched Penny deeply.

"I know now that God has forgiven me." Robin raised a tear-stained face. A look of joy shone through the sorrow in his eyes. "I feel it here in my heart." Solemnly he touched his chest.

"That's fine." Clyde purposely spoke matter-of-factly.

Robin rushed on: "The Lord has told me to confess to Dad and — " he paused awkwardly, "to Leonora. "Oh, I do hope they will forgive me!"

"Don't worry — they will," the doctor gave him a reassuring smile.

Quietly Penny slipped away. There was wonder in her face.

CHAPTER TWELVE

The staff dining room overlooked the side garden. The sun had already set; the mantle of night was fast descending upon the landscape. The oaks, now almost stripped of their leaves, were etched starkly against a gray sky.

Dr. Ashmore and Matron lingered over the sweet course. There was a look of anxiety on both their faces. Now and then they would glance expectantly toward the door, as if waiting for someone to enter at any moment.

"Poor woman!" Ruth was saying. "She was absolutely frantic. She looked just about ready to collapse. She had to be given a sedative."

"Mrs. Oosthuizen is still here then?"

Matron nodded. "I left her in the waiting room. I instructed a student nurse to keep an eye on her. Is there no chance that her husband will recover?"

The superintendent shook his head. "Not the slightest, I'm afraid." His lips pursed in a grim line. "He deserves to die!"

"I agree with you there. All the same, it's just as well the Lord doesn't deal with us according to what we deserve. Even now, should Oosthuizen regain consciousness and truly repent and turn to the Lord, he will be forgiven. In God's Word we read this precious promise — 'If we confess our sins, He is faithful and just to forgive us our sins and to cleanse us from all unrighteousness.' Remember the thief on the cross?"

Dr. Ashmore did not speak. He was drumming his fingers on the table, his brow furrowed in thought. Then he said slowly:

"Do you know, Ruth, I have witnessed many deaths, I have seen many tragic sights, but not one has affected me so deeply, has made such an impression upon me, as this accident of Oosthuizen's. The reason is that until quite recently I had not given eternity a single thought. Then how many of our doctors do? I must confess that I myself had grown quite hardened. But today, somehow, everything was different."

Dr. Ashmore paused. He took a quick glance at the door, then looking gravely at Ruth, he resumed: "I must also confess I had not given any special heed to a patient's cry of pain. People cry out in their delirium, in their anguish of body or mind. They are given a sedative or a drug, whichever the case may be. But today this thought struck me forcibly: There is no analgesic sufficiently strong to relieve a man or woman's mental torment. No tranquilizer can give complete peace of mind, no capsule can remove the burden of guilt. Only the Lord can remove that burden of guilt, only the Lord can restore harmony and balance to a soul bowed down with grief and despair. Today I saw it all so plainly — everything was made perfectly clear to me. It was like a revelation from the Lord Himself." He paused and smiled. "I have now accepted His salvation. The Lord Jesus has become my Saviour, too."

"Oh, Michael!" Ruth cried. Tears of gratitude and praise welled up in her eyes. "I'm so glad that at last you have seen the way. What a relief!" She sighed happily.

The dining room was swiftly emptying. One by one the doctors finished their meals, leaving either to return to their rota of duty or to go out for the evening.

Michael's long hand stretched across the table to clasp hers warmly.

"And all thanks to you," he said huskily. Ruth's heart glowed with delight.

The door opened abruptly and Clyde came striding toward their table. He sat down in the vacant chair. There were lines of strain around his mouth and eyes.

"Oosthuizen has gone. There was nothing more we could do for him, sir." Clyde turned almost apologetically to his chief.

Suddenly the intern buried his head in his hands. "I feel so helpless, so inadequate," he mumbled. "If only Oosthuizen had regained consciousness — even for a few minutes — I could have spoken to him about his soul. But now it's too late. Oosthuizen has gone to a Christless eternity." Clyde gave a long, weary sigh.

"Have some dinner, Clyde," Ruth suggested sympathetically. "You'll feel better afterwards. You're tired."

He raised his head and smiled wanly. "Thanks. But I don't think I could eat a thing."

"Try anyway." Ruth smiled encouragingly.

He smiled back. "All right — you win." And Clyde sampled the soup the waitress had set before him.

Ruth flashed Michael a significant glance. "Would you like to tell Clyde, or shall I?"

Questioningly the intern glanced at the chief, then at Matron. In his distress, he had not observed the radiance in her expressive eyes, or the deep emotion the superintendent was struggling to control.

Dr. Ashmore looked at Ruth who promptly remarked: "Something wonderful has happened, Clyde. I think you can guess."

He put down his spoon. He appeared slightly bemused.

"Our prayers have been answered, Clyde. Dr. Ashmore is now a believer. Not only does Doctor believe God is the Creator, but he has also put his trust in the Saviour."

Joy leaped into Clyde's eyes. "That's marvelous!"

Ruth went on: "It was this accident of Oosthuizen's that the Lord used finally to reveal the truth to Dr. Ashmore."

"That's right." The superintendent nodded. His smooth, controlled voice shook suspiciously. "Would you care to hear how it came about, Maxwell?"

Clyde nodded his head vigorously. "I would, sir. Very much." His despondency had vanished.

That morning, when Dr. Ashmore was visiting Casualty Ward, Oosthuizen had been admitted on a stretcher. Earlier in the day, he had assaulted and robbed a factory employee returning from the bank with the week's wages. Then, without arousing suspicion, he had managed to board a bus, the bag containing the stolen money clutched in his hand.

All might have gone well for the thief had not a policeman, in all innocence, been waiting at the bus stop where Oosthuizen had decided to get off. To his guilty conscience it must have seemed as if the law had caught up with him. In his panic, he had dashed blindly across the road, straight into a bus coming from the opposite direction.

"Divine justice," someone had exclaimed. Perhaps it was. The employee from the factory had been taken to Groote Schuur Hospital. Within an hour he had died from severe head injuries.

And now the thief himself was also dead.

Dr. Ashmore said: "It was hearing Oosthuizen shouting and

raving in his delirium that finally convinced me of man's need for regeneration — and of my own. Surgery can't give a man peace of mind. With medical skill we may be able to heal a man's body, but surgery can't save his soul. Drugs can to a certain extent relieve his physical pain and temporarily ease his tortured conscience. But capsules can't absolve him from his guilt. In a flash of revelation, I realized that the Lord Jesus alone can do that for mankind. Although I haven't done anything as bad or wicked as Oosthuizen, my life in God's sight — yes, my so-called respectable life — was in His eyes distasteful, as revolting as dirty, open sores in our eyes. God was not relevant in my life. My self-centered existence was repugnant to God. This morning I read in Isaiah 1:18, 'Though your sins be as scarlet, they shall be as white as snow; though they be red like crimson, they shall be as wool.' These words gripped my heart." Dr. Ashmore paused. There was a new air of serenity about him. "I can now echo with the Psalmist — 'He restoreth my soul . . . . '"

Smiling, Michael glanced from Clyde to Ruth. Deep contentment had replaced the unhappy expression in the Superintendent's eyes.

His companions nodded in joyous approval. Then Clyde began to quote from a well-known hymn:

> He breaks the power of cancelled sin,
> He sets the prisoner free,
> His blood can make the foulest clean
> His blood avails for me.

Ruth found she was unable to speak. In her heart there was a song of joy and gratitude to the Lord for all His goodness and mercy.

The next morning Penny arrived at the hospital earlier than usual, and when she entered the superintendent's office, she was surprised to see he was already there. He was bending over the filing cabinet.

"Good morning, Penny!" He turned to greet her affably. He was smiling one of his rare smiles.

"Good morning, Doctor." She sounded subdued, so different from her bright, cheerful self. He gave her a keen, professional scrutiny.

She was pale, there were shadows beneath her eyes and she looked as if she'd lost some weight. Compassion touched him.

Then next instant compunction mingled with compassion.

83

Yesterday he had remarked to Ruth and Clyde that he had not done anything so bad as Oosthuizen. But, Michael reprimanded himself severely, he had done far worse. He had destroyed a young girl's faith in God. The words of a certain text he had heard some Sundays ago flew into his mind with convicting clarity: "Whoso shall offend one of these little ones which believe in me, it were better for him that a millstone were hanged about his neck, and that he were drowned in the depths of the sea."

Suddenly Michael felt bogged down with grief.

But the Lord has cleansed me from my sin, he reminded himself. He had experienced what psychologists call "cataclysmic change," although psychology had not done that for him; Christ had done all. His self-righteousness could not make him a Christian. Only the power of God could bring about the miraculous change that had been wrought in his soul. Almost overnight everything had become new to him — new values, new desires, new attitudes and purposes.

Now, looking at Penny and perceiving the sadness, the near despair in her blue eyes, Dr. Ashmore resolved to do all in his power to restore her faith in God.

He reached out a tentative hand. "My dear, is anything troubling you?"

Her eyes evaded his scrutiny. "Why, no." Then, because she was not a clever dissembler, she exclaimed: "Oh, Doctor — Clyde told me this morning — I met him as I came in — and he said — he said — " Suddenly she was unable to continue.

"That I am now a believer. That is correct." Michael nodded, his eyes alight with a new happiness. "I have experienced a personal salvation — "

"I just can't understand it," she broke in. She stared at the doctor as if stricken. "It's incredible that you should now embrace the faith which previously you used to scorn so much."

With great effort she managed to quiet the tumult within her, to check herself from giving way to tears.

"No doubt it may seem so to you." He smiled at her. "Now let's get down to some work." He walked over to his desk and glanced down at the file in his hand. "Please get your notebook and pencil."

"Yes, Doctor," she responded, utter despair in her voice.

He was somewhat puzzled and perturbed by her odd reaction. Later in the day he would find an opportunity to have a chat with her. He decided she was probably having some trouble over her friendship with Anderson.

But as the day wore on, the chance to speak to Penny did not present itself. In the afternoon Dr. Ashmore was called to the operating theater, and at five o'clock she left the office without saying good-by to him.

In the car park she came face to face with the E.N.T. consultant.

"Hullo, Penny!" He grinned genially. "Haven't seen you all day." He paused, undecided. Then: "I find I have a free evening. How about coming out with me tonight?"

Penny looked dubious. With haunting persistence, Clyde's words of reproof still rang in her ears — "How could you encourage Anderson . . . when you have not the slightest intention of marrying the man? And how can you continue to use him as an escort when your motive is all wrong?"

Deliberately, almost fiercely, she pushed Clyde's words from her mind.

"Come on, Penny." Don took her arm possessively. He was smiling into her eyes. "You haven't been out with me for ages."

She felt tired and depressed and lonely, longing desperately for Michael's love.

"All right, Don — I'll come," she promised breathlessly.

"That's my girl." He took a quick glance around the car park. "I see you have your car here. I'll just go home and change and then come for you in say an hour's time. That suit you?"

She nodded, smiling and lovely in her smart winter outfit.

With a wave of her hand she stepped into her car and started the engine. She did not see a pair of warm brown eyes — eyes which at the moment expressed concern — watching her from a window in the left wing.

So Penny was still on very friendly terms with the E.N.T. consultant — perhaps she was even considering going out with him again.

Well, I guess it's none of my business. With a shrug Clyde Maxwell turned from the window and thrust his hands into the large pockets of his white surgical coat.

All the same, he wondered at the sudden ache in his heart.

CHAPTER THIRTEEN

Don helped Penny out of the car, his hand imprisoning hers as he led her toward the railing.

After dining in a Sea Point restaurant, he had steered the car along the winding road and up the pine-covered mountainside toward Signal Hill. The view from the top was breathtakingly beautiful.

Below them the city followed the curve of Table Bay. Lights twinkled through the darkness, large yellow lights marking the main roads. The beam from the lighthouse flashed intermittently across the bay, and the sky was clear and bright with moonlight. The air was still, like the brooding stillness of an impending storm.

Penny sniffed. "I smell the sea — and that means rain. Oh, how I hate the winters. I wish it were the beginning of spring and summer instead of winter."

"If you marry Old Ashmore it will be like being permanently married to winter."

Penny went pink with annoyance. "Who said anything about marrying Michael? And please don't refer to him as 'Old Ashmore.' You know I don't like it."

"All right — all right," Don muttered hastily. "Keep your wool on, old girl." He placed a caressing hand on her shoulder. "No offense meant."

Penny sighed. She should have refused to come out with him. She wasn't enjoying the evening at all. Her thoughts were on Michael — Michael and Ruth van Rhyn enjoying themselves somewhere — perhaps together at a meeting . . . perhaps discussing spiritual things over a cup of tea in Matron's private quarters.

"What's come over you, Penny?" Don's question jerked her out of her cogitations. "Lately you've been different."

"Have I?"

"You used to be such fun. We've had some grand times together." Don gave her shoulder an affectionate squeeze and drew her close to his side. "Come on, snap out of it and let's enjoy the rest of the evening. Have I told you? You look lovely. You're the most adorable girl I know." Swiftly he kissed the top of her head.

Tonight, because of the desolation in her heart, she was pleased at his attentions. It was good to know that at least one man admired her and found her desirable. All the same, she couldn't help wishing it were Michael at her side, Michael whispering endearing words in her ear, Michael giving her affectionate kisses.

Penny turned her gaze away from the bay. "I suppose you've heard that Dr. Ashmore is now a Christian?" She was unable to stop her question. She just had to discuss the subject with someone. All day it had preyed on her mind.

The E.N.T. surgeon nodded. "So I believe. But the chief wasn't exactly a heathen before, you know." Don's eyes teased her.

"He was an agnostic. And that's tantamount to being a heathen."

"I've heard that you're also an agnostic," Don put in. "Is that correct?"

She nodded briefly. "But that surely doesn't make me a heathen? Or does it? Oh, no!" Her distress showed plainly in her face. "Oh, I just don't know!" She knotted her hands in a gesture of despair.

He caught hold of her hands and kissed them with simulated fervor.

"Don't let that worry you, my sweet. You're too young and lovely to bother your pretty head about religion." She looked so vulnerable, so untouched. "Forget about old Ashmore — pardon me! — and let's concentrate on ourselves. What if he has been converted? It shouldn't concern us anyway."

"It concerns me a great deal," Penny told Don, pulling her hands free.

"Why, are you considering becoming a Christian too?" Don's eyes were upon her, bright and mocking.

"That's not funny! You know I wouldn't consider the idea. I'm thinking of Matron, of what this latest development could mean to her. She and Michael will become more friendly than ever — he might even ask her to marry him."

Don intercepted with a laugh. "Surely you're not jealous of Matron? My dear girl, how could any man look at Ruth van Rhyn, even glance at her when you're in the picture? You're so sweet, my darling Penny. And I adore you."

Don's voice changed suddenly. It was no longer mocking, but husky with desire. His eyes burned with a strange light.

His arms tightened about her. Then he was kissing her, his lips warm and demanding against her mouth.

Swiftly she backed away from him. She liked Don best when he was in one of his laughing, bantering moods. She was always a little afraid of him when he became too intense, too ardent. She wanted their relationship to remain on a happy, carefree level. She didn't want to become serious with him.

Headlights flashed. Cars came cautiously around the sharp bend in the road.

"Come on — " firmly Don took her arm, "let's drive further down."

He opened the car door for her to get in, slid behind the steering wheel and reached to take off the handbrake. Then he let in the clutch, reversed the car and drove down the hillside the way they had come.

Without any difficulty, so it seemed to Penny, he found a parking place between the pines, just as if he were familiar with all the right spots. Table Mountain rose sharply before them, awesome and eerie and forbidding in the darkness.

Penny felt Don's shoulder against hers. She let him rest there. Suddenly she was too weary, too wrapped up in her emotions to move.

Abruptly he spoke. "Still thinking of the chief?" When Penny deigned no reply, he added, "You're too young, too sweet to throw yourself away on someone like Ashmore. He wouldn't appreciate you. Now I would." Don's eyes burned into hers with an intensity which startled her.

"Isn't it time to go home?" She regretted her impetuous arrangement to go out with him. But to sit at home and brood, to dwell on Michael — perhaps enjoying himself with Ruth —

"Tired of me already?" There was reproach in Don's voice.

"Not exactly . . . I'm not in the mood tonight."

"You never are these days. What's biting you? You used to be such fun."

His arms went around her. His sudden kiss was passionate and somehow distasteful.

88

"Please let me go! I want to go home."

"Dear me!" His voice mocked her. But she could tell from his dark expression that he was angry and frustrated.

Don, with his strong streak of vanity and desire to dominate, was always confident of his powers to charm. The nurses at the hospital fell over him in their desire to please him. They fed his vanity. But not so Penny — this small, sweet girl who was the chief's secretary. She was enslaved by Michael Ashmore. Her mind was completely under his domination and there seemed so little Don could do about it.

During the past weeks he had deliberately avoided the girl, hoping she would miss him, and when this evening she had consented to come out with him, he was determined to persuade her to become his wife. So far his efforts to charm her had met only with amusement, his passion with reproach and a cold fear. Not exactly flattering!

It called for a new form of approach, a new strategy.

He took her small, cold hand in his own and caressed it gently. His smiling eyes masked his anger, his humiliation.

"Dear, sweet Penny — what a brute you must think me! I want to marry you, my darling. Now don't refuse me before you have considered the matter carefully." He silenced her lips with a tender kiss.

With a deft movement she wrenched herself free.

"Why do you want to marry me?" she shot unexpectedly at him.

"Why?" Don was momentarily nonplussed.

She peered at him accusingly. "You haven't told me you love me. Not once have you said so."

He affected a laugh. "Why, of course I love you! You dear, sweet, silly girl. Fancy thinking I don't love you. Here, let me prove it to you." He drew her swiftly into his arms and began kissing her with fervor.

She did not respond. Instead she once more jerked away from him.

"Kissing doesn't prove a thing. I should imagine you'd find it very easy to kiss a girl."

Penny was proving difficult, stubborn and willful. She was not such an easy catch as he had fondly believed. Under her sweetness there was great determination. She knew her own mind, and her mind was set on becoming Mrs. Michael Ashmore. Don failed to understand what she could possibly see in the man. In his opinion his chief was a cold-blooded fish. Good looking, no doubt, but too caustic, too ascetic, and certainly far too detached and reserved. A typical introvert, Dr. Ashmore was definitely not a suitable partner for a warm, impulsive girl like Penny. He would suit Matron far better.

"I find it very easy to kiss you, Penny," Don countered, smiling. Once more he attempted to take her in his arms.

"No! Please let me go. I have no intention of marrying you. I've told you that so many times. I would like to continue to be friends with you. That's all I want, Don — just friendship. Can't we leave it at that?"

His face set in sullen lines. "So you've just been playing with my feelings, like some cheap little flirt?" His tone was full of injured pride.

"Don't say that," came her cold retort. "I've not been playing with your feelings. No one can accuse me of that."

"Then what do you call it, I'd like to know?" he demanded, no longer able to conceal his annoyance, no longer bothering to exercise his charm. "If you had no intention of becoming my wife, then why did you lead me on?"

Penny was silent. Again Clyde Maxwell's words came to her — "How could you encourage Anderson . . . when you have not the slightest intention of marrying the man?"

"I — " She moistened her lips. She was trembling now, partly from shame, partly from panic. She had not seen Don so angry as now. Michael had warned her of the E.N.T. surgeon's temper.

He deserves to be furious, Penny told herself. *I haven't played fair with him.* She had been unwise and foolish. But not really wicked. Not for a moment did she believe that Don loved her. He was too fond of himself to care deeply for anyone.

Then no harm has been done, Penny tried to reassure herself, brushing aside Clyde's words of rebuke. But what if it had been some other man — someone who really cared for her? Could she then have used him to make Michael jealous? The thought that perhaps she was a sinner was suddenly frightening.

She endeavored a smile. "I deny that I've been leading you on. To you, love is just a game. I'm quite sure you've been taking out several girls besides me."

This Don repudiated with force. "I have not! I've been concentrating on you, fondly thinking that you felt the same as I did. That you wanted marriage."

"But," she protested impatiently, "Surely I've made it perfectly clear to you that that's not the case — "

He intervened with scorn: "You just wanted a gay time — a charming escort, some silly sucker who'd be quite willing to string along with you. Well, that's not me! You have to make up your mind once and for all. Either you agree to marry me, or it's all off between us."

"I didn't know there was anything between us," she murmured a little lamely, "except friendship, that is. Somehow I had the idea that you're keen on Staff Nurse Gregory. So why not ask her to become your wife? I'm quite certain you'd find her more than willing to oblige."

"We'll leave Phyl out of this, if you don't mind." Don was scowling at Penny. An impulse to slap her face was strong and demanding. "At least she knows how to conduct herself when she is out with a man."

Penny's stormy eyes matched his. "I wouldn't marry you if you were the last man on earth!" she flung at him childishly.

Don stared at Penny with dismay. Not for a moment had he anticipated such a tempestuous reaction. But even in her anger, she somehow managed to look sweet and appealing, so touchingly young and naive.

His vanity had received a sharp blow. But he could not — he would not believe she really meant what she said.

He was filled with a quick longing to assert the same mastery as Michael Ashmore had over her emotions.

Before she could protest, he had seized her hands and was kissing them with an ardor which left her breathless.

"Please — Don — !" Her blue eyes grew wide with apprehension.

"Sorry." He released her hands as if with reluctance. "But I can't let you go. Please give me a chance."

His voice sounded unreal to his ears. He, Don Anderson — handsome, charming, a gifted consultant — who could have almost any woman he wanted, pleading with a girl to give him a chance. It went against the grain, against his pride. But pride had to take a back seat where money was involved. Once they were safely married —

With bitterness a similar occasion was called to mind. Only then it was Phyl who had pleaded with him. His lips twisted ironically.

"I'm sorry, Don." Penny sounded genuinely apologetic. "I'd no idea you cared for me quite so much. I see now that it was quite wrong of me to encourage you."

"So you admit you've encouraged me?" he asked, an aggrieved note in his voice.

"In that case — yes. I guess I should have told you straight out when I knew of your intentions. But I was flattered," she admitted ruefully. "And perhaps lonely. You see, I wanted to make Michael — "

"Forget Ashmore!" Don told her forcibly. "What's the use of wasting your life dreaming of him? If the chief ever decides to marry — and somehow I don't think he will — it will probably be to Matron or to someone equally old and staid. You can take it from me," the E.N.T. consultant added maliciously, "that Ashmore has no matrimonial ideas regarding you, my dear, sweet, little Penny."

"Oh!" She drew a sharp, disappointed breath. "That was cruel of you, Don."

He smiled placatingly. "One has sometimes to be cruel to be kind."

"Take me home — I'm tired." She felt emotionally and physically exhausted.

He gave her a sharp, professional scrutiny. She certainly looked worn-out, not at all like her healthy, happy self.

"Would you like me to give you a capsule or something to make you sleep?" he questioned with concern.

"No thanks." She shook her head decisively. "I'm not that desperate — yet."

"Then I suggest you forget old Ashmore. No good can come of such an infatuation."

Hastily she refuted Don's suggestion. "I love Michael — and I don't care who knows it." She raised grave, ingenuous eyes to his. "Now please take me home."

Don gave an exasperated sigh as he started the car.

They hardly exchanged a word on the drive back. Penny was miserable and forlorn; the evening hadn't gone quite as she had expected. Perhaps she should have responded to Don's advances instead of allowing Clyde's solemn words to influence her and so spoil her enjoyment of the evening. She had looked to Don to lift her out of her depression, her loneliness, but things hadn't worked out that way.

Later, as she climbed into bed, she had to admit that it was Clyde's reproving words, and not her love for Michael, that had prevented her from having fun with Don.

92

CHAPTER FOURTEEN

During the next few days Penny deliberately avoided her chief whenever possible. Quietly she attended to her work, without her usual comments and smiling observations. Whether Dr. Ashmore was aware of her new reserve, her pensive expression, Penny couldn't say. There was about him an air of happiness — a joy which he neither attempted to suppress nor to conceal. A secret smile lurked on his lips, and his eyes, when he looked at Ruth van Rhyn, held an expression Penny found difficult to fathom. It was an expression which chilled her heart and filled her with dark forebodings.

She also kept out of Don Anderson's way. That was fairly easy, for it was not often that she had contact with him. Occasionally he dictated an urgent letter which Penny obligingly typed for him. The consultants had their own typists, but whenever a letter required immediate attention, they had a habit of coming to Penny to help them out. This the superintendent did not appear to mind, so long as his secretary kept her own work up to date and there was no interference with his routine.

And as for Clyde Maxwell, Penny's thoughts were somewhat mixed and confused. She found she was becoming increasingly aware of him, feeling subconsciously that in some way or other he would be able to sort out her confusion. With some relief she recalled his promise to help if ever she were in any spiritual difficulty.

Suddenly he loomed before her. He came striding along the corridor, white surgical coat flapping, his reading glasses sticking out of his large pocket, stethoscope slung round his neck.

A typical young intern, Penny mused, flashing him a smile.

93

"Hullo, Penny! Sorry I can't stay to talk. I'm due to assist in theater. A tracheotomy case."

A boy of four, Ronnie Briggs, had just been admitted to Casualty Ward. While playing with his sister's bracelet, he had pushed up his nostril one of the plastic charms which had come loose. The charm was now sitting in the patient's trachea and he had to have artificial breathing. Clyde had immediately alerted the E.N.T. surgeon, who had to abandon his operating list in this crisis.

Clyde had now completed his stretch on Casualty. For the next few months he was to assist in theater; then, as intern to one of the consultants, he would have a spell on the wards. In a way, it was a relief from stitching cuts in Casualty.

Now, booted, gowned and masked, his hands scrubbed and gloved, the intern stood waiting on the side of the operating table, the anesthetist on the other. Under the theater supervisor's direction, a staff and student nurse lifted the young patient to the table under the great, powerful lights. To assist the boy's breathing, a tube was suspended to his windpipe.

As the theater staff nurse was off duty, Phyl Gregory had been alerted to fill her place. Now, holding her feelings in stern check, she tensely waited for the E.N.T. surgeon to enter the operating theater.

Suddenly he was there, looking grim and serious, which he usually did when he was set on business. No longer was he the gay and charming playboy. He was a surgeon employing all his knowledge and skill, earnestly fighting to save a life from physical death.

Whether he recognized her or not, Staff Nurse Gregory could not tell. He certainly gave no sign of it as she helped him with his gown and smoothed on his gloves. As always, he was intent upon the job at hand, and for this she could admire him. She had missed seeing much of him, as lately her rota of duty did not frequently coincide with his.

Don Anderson certainly knows his job, Clyde reflected, noting the adept manner in which the E.N.T. specialist went about the intricate surgery.

The operation was a complete success, of that there was not the slightest doubt. The patient's life was saved; soon he would be able to dispense with artificial breathing. Meanwhile he was to be kept in the oxygen tent.

Inwardly Clyde offered a prayer of praise and thankfulness.

94

He would always be grateful to the Lord for allowing him the privilege of taking part in this great ministry of healing. But the healing of a soul was in the Lord's eyes infinitely more precious.

The intern went along to the children's surgical ward and instructed the nurse on duty to get the intravenous stand ready at Ronnie's bedside. He would be coming later to fix the saline drip.

The nurse in charge of the ward was off duty until five p.m. so Clyde guessed correctly that Staff Nurse Gregory would be serving the surgeon with tea in the office.

As he passed the doorway, he heard Phyl Gregory call out in a friendly voice: "Have some tea, Dr. Maxwell."

He stood undecided. It was jolly decent of Phyl Gregory to offer him tea. The staff nurses did not as a rule have much time for struggling young interns. Most of the senior nurses went all out to please the consultants and visiting physicians and surgeons.

Clyde was about to step into the office when he noticed Don Anderson's expression. He did not appear exactly pleased. So Clyde shook his head and, thanking her, he swiftly disappeared down a side corridor.

Usually Clyde did not pay much attention to the hospital grapevine. In the staff dining room he would occasionally overhear his colleagues discussing one of the nurses, especially if the girl in question happened to be good looking. The grapevine had it that Staff Gregory was keen on the E.N.T. surgeon, but Anderson's interests were elsewhere engaged. On Penny Fielding, no doubt. Since that afternoon he had seen her and Anderson chatting together in the car park, Clyde had frequently wondered how their courtship — if any — were progressing, whether the consultant had made any headway with her, or whether the girl's heart and mind were still set on marrying Dr. Ashmore, to whom she was so obviously devoted.

Suddenly Clyde was aware of an overwhelming desire to know what had transpired between Penny and Anderson. The other morning when he caught a glimpse of her, she had looked pale and dejected. Poor Penny! How he yearned to help her. Was she brooding over Anderson — or was it Dr. Ashmore's conversion that had caused her to grieve, thinking that now the chief would automatically turn to Ruth? Clyde wished he knew.

Meanwhile, Phyl was glancing at Don with unconcealed admiration shining from her eyes.

"You were wonderful," she was saying in a hushed, awed voice, as she poured him a second cup of tea. "Absolutely wonderful! You have great ability, Don. You'll reach the top yet."

"Ah, that depends." He flung her a shrewd look. "Now, if I'd money behind me — "

"Not necessarily. Money isn't everything. Money with the wrong kind of wife can be an obstacle, a hindrance instead of an asset. How — how are things between you and Penny? Have you made any progress with her?" Phyl ventured, hardly daring to glance at him.

The surgeon laughed harshly and set down his cup.

"Off! Completely off. Not that there was anything ever on. It was ambition only that made me seek her out in the first place. But the sweet little dear has her heart set on marrying the chief. What a hope she has! He wouldn't look twice at an immature little kid like Penny. She doesn't know the first thing about love. Not like you, Phyl."

The consultant paused and looked searchingly at the staff nurse. At that moment she appeared to him more beautiful than he could ever remember. Her eyes shone with a soft light; her whole face reflected the ardent love which burned within her. *A sight for tired eyes,* he mused, admiring again her tall, beautifully molded figure, the golden hair, the kissable lips. He had been a fool to push Phyl to one side for the sake of Penny Fielding's money.

He reached out to take the staff nurse's hand. But she demurred: "Not here, Don. I'm off tonight," she suggested. "I could meet you then."

The surgeon nodded with satisfaction. "Good! So am I. Let's make a date."

Then, having settled the time and place, he went on to detail the various treatments he wanted given to his patients.

"And tell night nurse to keep Ronnie Briggs well sedated throughout the night," the consultant added. "Now I shall write up the post-operative sedatives. And see that everything is charted, Staff Nurse."

The surgeon spoke curtly but the expression in his eyes set her pulse racing.

"Very good, Dr. Anderson," Phyl responded in her best professional voice. She couldn't wait for the evening to arrive quickly enough!

* * * * * * * *

The E.N.T. consultant and Staff Nurse Gregory were engaged to be married. The hospital was agog with the news the next day. Young doctors who had their eye on the staff nurse shrugged philosophically; the nurses who had cherished secret dreams shed a few secret tears.

The superintendent and Matron were discussing the latest admittance to the hospital — an orthopedic case, a young teen-ager — when Ruth suddenly remembered to mention Phyl and Don's engagement.

"I must confess I'm relieved," Ruth added, smiling across at Michael. "Now that Anderson is engaged to Staff Gregory, there is less chance of Penny becoming involved with him."

Dr. Ashmore did not return Matron's smile. He nodded gravely.

"In a way I'm glad. But what of Penny's feelings for Anderson? How do you think she'll take the news? Lately she's been looking far from happy." Michael's frown betrayed his anxiety for the girl.

"You needn't worry about Penny's feelings for Anderson," Ruth hastened to assure the superintendent. "I doubt whether she — "

The ringing of the telephone cut short the rest of her sentence, and when Dr. Ashmore replaced the receiver, the subject of Penny was completely shelved in the face of an emergency that had arisen in the orthopedic ward.

The superintendent spoke briskly to Matron. "You're wanted in orthopedics to settle a dispute. That was Nurse Cooper on the line. Apparently the new patient, Sylvia Blackwell, threw a cup of scalding tea in the ward aide's face. Miss Hopkins has been admitted to Casualty for treatment. She fainted from shock — she's not exactly robust, I'm afraid." Dr. Ashmore paused. "Perhaps I'd better come along with you to restore law and order. It looks as if we're going to have a spot of bother with young Blackwell. These modern teen-agers — " and the superintendent shrugged significantly. "Many of them make the nurses' lives a misery. No respect for their elders — no manners whatsoever — lacking in discipline and self-control — "

Despite the seriousness of the situation, Ruth smiled.

"Oh, they're not as bad as some people think. We have some exceptionally fine teen-agers in the Youth Fellowship at church."

"Then it's a pity more teen-agers don't consider joining the church. That should keep them well out of mischief."

In the past Dr. Ashmore frequently had made that particular

observation. But then it had been spoken in sarcasm. Now Ruth saw from his expression that the comment was given in all earnestness. She praised the Lord afresh for saving the soul of the man she loved.

Penny heard the news of the E.N.T. consultant's engagement to Staff Nurse Gregory when helping to serve tea in the pediatric ward. This she would sometimes volunteer to do on her afternoons off.

Today her motive was purely selfish. She dreaded going home, dreaded spending another evening alone with her tormented thoughts. Perhaps she should not have sent Don Anderson packing. Now she had no one — absolutely no one. Michael did not pay much attention to her. He was wrapped up in his work, in his new spiritual life — and in Matron, Penny added bitterly. She could not recall feeling bitter about anyone before.

Mechanically she took a mug from the cart.

"Only half a mug for Baby Brenda," a student nurse called out.

Penny smiled sympathetically at the young patient who eagerly extended a pair of chubby arms.

"Here you are, dear." Firmly Penny held on to the mug. The child gurgled happily as she drank her tea.

The nurse resumed her conversation with her colleague. Their voices came clearly to Penny's ears.

"So at last Staff Gregrory has managed to get herself engaged. And to that handsome consultant, of all people. Some girls have all the luck —"

Penny spun round. "Who's engaged to be married? I couldn't help overhearing — " She gestured eloquently with her free hand.

"Staff Gregory."

"Oh, I mustn't forget to congratulate her. And who is the young man?"

"The E.N.T. surgeon, Miss Fielding."

"Really." Penny knew a swift stab of hurt, of disappointment. She couldn't say exactly why she should be disappointed to hear of Don's engagement. She didn't love him. In the beginning, it was true, she had been somewhat fond of him and had enjoyed his attentions. It added to a girl's esteem to have an escort, especially such a good-looking one as the E.N.T. surgeon.

Her pride had received a sharp blow. Only a few days ago he had with much passion declared his love for her. Now here he was engaged to Phyl Gregory.

The fickleness of men! Penny thought in disgust.

She returned to her office for her coat. Acute loneliness assailed her. The superintendent was not in his office. The window was open, a cold wind ruffling the curtains.

The weather was changing rapidly. The sun had disappeared. Cold, dark clouds were chasing one another across the gray sky. The air smelled like rain. She drew the collar of her coat around her.

She should be on her way. But what was there to go home to? Suddenly she missed her father, missed him far more acutely than she had done in the earlier days.

That was because she and Michael had now grown apart. And for that she had to thank Ruth van Rhyn, who had taken Michael away from her.

"Oh, Michael!" The cry broke involuntarily from her lips. She felt an urgent need for sympathy. She was hungry for love, for companionship.

Tears of self-pity, of humiliation, of utter desolation welled up in her blue eyes. And then the strain, the sleeplessness, the despondency from which she had suffered since hearing of Michael's conversion to Christianity, were released in a torrent of tears, which she made no effort to restrain.

She did not hear the opening door, did not hear the superintendent step into his office, did not hear his gentle question.

She was weeping as if her heart were breaking.

There arose within him a strong desire to console the girl. No doubt she had just learned of Anderson's engagement to Staff Gregory. So Penny did love that young surgeon after all.

His own part, that part he had played in her life which had caused her to lose her faith, came to him again with a swift contrition. It was up to him to make amends, to do what he could to win this girl to the Lord, to restore her faith in God.

Tomorrow was Sunday. He was free in the morning and would arrange to take her with him to church.

He placed a compassionate hand on her shoulder. "Don't cry, my pet." He spoke soothingly, using the endearment he had called her when she was a child.

She became aware of him then. With a cry, she buried her head against his chest.

"Oh — Michael," she gulped between her sobs. "I'm so miserable! So unhappy!"

"There, there." His long arms went around her. "I'm here to

help you, Penny. There's no need to cry, you know. I understand," he whispered gently.

"You do?" She gazed up at him, her eyes red and swollen, her
face flushed and feverish.

He put a hand to her hot brow and, with a tenderness almost
foreign to him, smoothed back her chestnut hair.

The telephone rang, but for once he ignored it.

"Come on, Penny, I'll drive you home. You're not in a fit state
to drive yourself."

"No — please — Michael — I don't want to go home! It's so
lonely. I couldn't bear it!" And with an agonizing moan, she
once more buried her face against his chest.

His nearness caused her heart to pound so much that she found
breathing almost a pain.

As she swayed, the doctor's arms tightened about the discon-
solate girl in a desperate attempt to soothe and to comfort her.

His back was to the office door which led into the main corridor. The door had been left ajar. Neither saw the door swing
open, the startled dismay in Matron's expressive eyes, the quick
closing of the door as Ruth speedily returned to her own office.

CHAPTER FIFTEEN

Ruth van Rhyn, Matron of Oakhurst Hospital, stood at the window looking out, seeing not the winter sunshine on the lush green lawns and bare oak trees, but seeing the superintendent, Dr. Ashmore, holding Penny Fielding in his arms.

The picture had remained in her mind since the day she had gone into his office and had seen him embracing Penny.

The extremely cold weather had come and gone. The wind and rain had lasted almost a fortnight. Today was calm and golden and warm, but Ruth's heart knew a strange coldness — a coldness she was finding exceedingly difficult to shrug away.

She moved from the window as someone knocked on her office door. In response to her "Come in," Clyde Maxwell entered and closed the door behind him.

"Hullo, Clyde." She was always glad to see the young intern whom she had known since he was a lad of four and she a schoolgirl of fourteen.

"I'm afraid Penny won't be coming with us to the meeting this evening," Ruth told the house doctor with regret.

"Oh." Quickly he veiled his expression, but not before she had seen his sharp disappointment.

"I'm sorry, Clyde." Ruth beckoned to him to take a seat.

He grinned philosophically and sat down.

"Well, I had hoped she'd come along with us even though the chief couldn't make it," he admitted ruefully after a small silence.

"So had I. But — " Ruth shrugged. It seemed to her that Penny was not at all interested in coming to church unless Dr. Ashmore was free to take her.

"I was beginning to hope she was keen to attend church and meetings for her own spiritual good," Clyde couldn't help but voice his anxious thoughts. "Not only for the sake of being in the chief's company."

Unconsciously Ruth let out a sigh. The morning after she had seen Michael and Penny together, she had not been able to accompany them to church as she was on duty. In the afternoon when she had telephoned Penny to inquire whether she would like to come with Clyde and herself to the evening service, the girl had curtly refused the invitation. She had sounded almost hostile, Ruth remembered. On the next Wednesday evening they had all gone together in the superintendent's large car to the midweek Bible study. Penny, practically ignoring Ruth, but smiling at Clyde, had gone to sit in the front seat with Michael, who had given Ruth an apologetic smile.

Then last Sunday Dr. Ashmore had not been free to take Penny to the morning service. Ruth, who was off duty, had gladly offered, but once more Penny had declined the invitation.

Now it was Wednesday again.

"Do you think the chief has been able to make any headway with Penny?" Clyde questioned. He added quickly: "In relation to spiritual things, I mean."

"I couldn't say. I haven't seen much of Dr. Ashmore lately — and we haven't discussed Penny."

Something in her tone caused the intern to ask: "Is anything the matter, Ruth? I'm not trying to pry — I'm really concerned." He shifted a little awkwardly in his seat. "You and the chief were becoming such great friends."

A gentle flush suffused her cheeks.

Hastily Clyde said: "I'm sorry — Perhaps I shouldn't have asked you."

"That's all right," she assured him. "I must confess I'm a little worried over Penny's attitude. I'm going to speak freely to you, Clyde. She seems to regard me as a sort of rival."

He nodded briefly. "So I've noticed. She seems very much in love with the chief. I have an idea she resents your friendship with him. But she needn't worry — in fact, I told her so."

"When was this?" Ruth's calm voice surprised her.

Clyde considered a moment. "It was that first Sunday Dr. Ashmore took you to church. Penny was worrying herself sick in case the chief should turn to you. I assured her she had nothing to fear from you, that your only concern was to help the chief spiritually, that you had no romantic interest in him whatsoever."

102

Ruth was silent. Then she said: "I'm afraid I shall have to disillusion you, Clyde."

He stared at her in amazement. "You don't mean to say — "

She nodded. "I do, Clyde. I love Michael Ashmore. I have loved him for fourteen long years. I hope I haven't shocked you, but I couldn't let you go on believing — well, a lie."

"You haven't shocked me, Ruth. I'm surprised, that's all. I had no idea — And all these years you have been praying for him to come to the Lord. And now your prayers have been answered. The chief is no longer an agnostic, but a believer. And now he is trying to get Penny interested in spiritual things."

Thoughtfully Ruth tapped her pen on the blotting-paper on her desk.

"Penny is very much on Dr. Ashmore's conscience. He was instrumental in her losing whatever faith she had. I think I've mentioned that to you before. Now he's doing his utmost to win her for the Lord. He's even giving her private Bible lessons — he has studied quite a number of books dealing with medical science and the Scriptures and he knows his subject pretty thoroughly by now. But whether he's making any headway with her, it's difficult to say. Perhaps God is speaking to her and she is afraid to yield in case it would mean the end of her seeing so much of Doctor. She is thoroughly enjoying her new role."

"Hm." Clyde's eyes were reflective. "Do you think — that is — have you any idea of the chief's feelings for Penny?" His question came a little diffidently.

Ruth hesitated, visualizing again the scene of Michael embracing Penny.

"Doctor is not one to reveal his feelings easily, as you doubtless know. But from what I have observed I should think he must care for her a little, if not a great deal."

"Hm." Clyde sounded crestfallen. His pleasant face was grave. "So now it's just a question of time before she'll become Mrs. Michael Ashmore."

Silence fell between Matron and the intern — a silence of mutual understanding and sympathy.

Briskly Ruth said: "About tonight, Clyde. Shall I meet you as usual?"

"Thanks, Ruth." He paused. "Soon I'll be able to give you a lift sometime. I'm saving hard for a car."

"Good!" She smiled fondly at him. "I see from the rota that you're not on call this long weekend. Going home to Leonora?"

"Yes. I'm looking forward to seeing Robin again. According to Leonora, he's settling down splendidly."

"So I've heard. Your sister rang me yesterday to invite me to spend the weekend with her. But I'm afraid I was unable to accept." Ruth's fine brows drew together in thought. "I have an idea. Why not ask Penny to go along with you?"

"Penny! No, I couldn't do that — "

"Why not? Leonora would be delighted to have her, I'm sure. It will do Penny a world of good to get away for a break. Think it over, Clyde."

A knock sounded on the door. Both looked up as the door opened to reveal the tall, slim figure of the medical superintendent.

Instantly Clyde rose to his feet.

"No, don't go, Maxwell. I've just come to tell you and Matron that I'm free this evening after all. The medical meeting has been postponed till next week. Now, shall we all go in my car or would you rather — "

"I'll go on my own," Clyde volunteered at once. "But thanks all the same, Dr. Ashmore."

"What about Penny?" Ruth inquired, not looking at the doctor.

"Penny told me earlier that she wasn't free this evening. So I presume she has something else on."

"Don't you think," Ruth suggested promptly, "that we should ask her again? She may have changed her mind — maybe she'll be glad to come with us."

Quietly Clyde slipped out of the office. Dr. Ashmore sat down.

"No!" The superintendent's tone was emphatic. "I'd rather we didn't. To tell the truth, I'd welcome a break from Penny tonight." He frowned and stroked back his smooth, blond hair. "I'm finding it somewhat difficult trying to teach that young lady. She just won't concentrate. I wish you'd take it on, Ruth."

He looked harassed and perplexed, so unlike his cool, confident self. Her heart went out to him in quick sympathy.

She smiled. "I'd willingly do so. But I'm afraid Penny wouldn't take kindly to the idea."

"Yes, you're right." He sighed and Ruth's discerning gaze was swift to note the strained look in his steel-gray eyes.

"I've missed you lately," he suddenly remarked, giving her a keen glance.

"We've both been busy, Michael." Ruth's reply came steadily, though her pulses were fluttering.

Dr. Ashmore resumed: "Maxwell said he would be going on his own. How about having supper with me first?"

"That would be lovely, Michael." Ruth couldn't conceal the radiance in her expressive eyes.

"How soon could you be ready after five? Would half an hour do for you to change and dress?"

She nodded, scarcely daring to glance at him for fear of revealing the love which she was sure was mirrored in her eyes.

When the superintendent returned to his office, he found Penny anxiously waiting for him.

"Oh, Doctor — I've changed my mind," she told him in a breathless voice. "I shall be coming with you tonight to the church meeting."

He narrowed his eyes and stared at her with something like dismay.

"I thought you'd be pleased." Her voice held an aggrieved note.

He passed a baffled hand across his brow.

"You told me you were otherwise engaged this evening." He paused and directed her a sharp look. "By the way, how do you know I'll be going to the Bible Study this evening? As far as you knew, there was that medical meeting I had to attend."

"I couldn't help overhearing you on the telephone," Penny spoke in a small voice. "That meeting has been cancelled, so now I presume you are free to attend church. May I come with you, Michael?" She gazed imploringly up at him.

"All right." His retort was curt. "Now run along to your own office and close the door."

The superintendent spoke briskly over the intercom. "Ruth — I'm sorry about this evening. Penny will be coming with us after all. Do you mind?"

"Of course not, Michael." A slight pause. Then: "What about our supper appointment?"

"Would you mind if we postponed it? Perhaps some other time when Penny is not with us."

"That will be fine." Ruth tried not to sound hurt or disappointed, but for once her voice gave her away.

Frowning, the doctor turned to the paper work on his desk. But he failed to concentrate. He was sure he had detected a note of hurt in Ruth's voice.

During the past few weeks he had perceived a slight change in her attitude toward him. She was still friendly, though a new reserve had entered their relationship.

Before his interest in spiritual things, they had scarcely been aware of each other. He couldn't speak for Ruth, of course. But where he was concerned, he couldn't ever recall giving her a second glance or thought. She had been there — a necessary asset to the hospital, part of the hospital equipment, as the saying went. He had taken her presence for granted. But since his conversion — here Michael smiled inwardly — he had become conscious of her in a way he had not previously been conscious of any woman. She affected him as no other had ever done. He wanted to be near her constantly. Her happiness meant his happiness. Her hurt, her disappointment caused him to feel for her deeply.

Suddenly he let out a low exclamation. And on his face was the look of one who had made an astonishing discovery.

CHAPTER SIXTEEN

It was wonderful walking through the wooded avenue with Clyde. Penny could not recall enjoying herself so much with anyone for a long time. Not even with Michael. With him she so often felt tongue tied and unsure of herself. But with Clyde she was poised and self-assured, instinctively knowing that he respected her. He treated her as an equal and not as some silly, immature girl who had to be humored. And barely tolerated, she added to herself a trifle bitterly.

Penny drew a deep breath, eagerly embracing the invigorating air. The sun, filtering through the trees, was warm on their backs; the sky above was clear and blue.

"It was jolly decent of your sister to invite me to spend this long weekend here at Constantia. It was good of you to think of me, Clyde."

"Glad you're enjoying yourself," he responded a little uncertainly. "Though actually it was Ruth's idea — "

Penny stopped walking. She stared hard at her companion.

"What's wrong?" Clyde turned to her in concern.

Penny's eyes sparkled with annoyance. "So Ruth wanted me out of the way. No doubt so that she could have Michael all to herself. Oh, why was I such a fool! And I thought you were my friend, Clyde." There was reproach in Penny's voice — a reproach which stung.

He had an absurd desire to take her in his arms, to kiss those pouting lips, to tell her not to bother her head with the superintendent and Matron. But he did none of these things.

He heard himself saying: "Ruth thought it would do you good to have a break. And I agreed. We both had your interest at heart. Her suggestion had nothing whatever to do with trying to get you away from the chief, of that I'm quite positive. Besides, you were free this weekend — you wouldn't have seen much of the chief, anyway."

"He would have taken me to church tomorrow," Penny countered swiftly.

"Not necessarily. He might not be free to attend morning service. I'll be taking you tomorrow, Penny." Clyde's gaze upon her was oddly tender. "To both services, if you like. Leonora has offered me the loan of her car."

Immediately Penny was contrite. "Sorry for my outburst, Clyde." She smiled suddenly — a sweet, shy smile.

He allowed his eyes to wander over her face, her form. Her face was flushed and glowing with healthy exercise. She was clad in a simple jumper suit which enhanced her slim, girlish figure.

She is really a most charming girl, he decided.

Penny, in spite of her wealth, was quite unsophisticated and unworldly. Modern, yes, but not fashion conscious. She was a girl Clyde could admire and love. But, he reminded himself, Penny was not a Christian. Also she had made it perfectly clear to him that Dr. Ashmore was the beginning and end of her existence. He was her whole world.

There's not a chance for me, the intern told himself with a resigned shrug. *Not a hope.*

She was looking much happier and prettier these days; in fact, she had been ever since the superintendent had started to take her with him to church. Clyde was painfully aware, however, that her radiant happiness was due solely to the fact that she was able to be with her beloved doctor. The church attendance itself had made no difference to her. She went about her duties at the hospital locked in her world of dreams, her eyes shining like stars, her radiant face reflecting her ardent love.

Surely listening to the Gospel message must have made some sort of impact upon her by now. Could Ruth possibly be right, Clyde asked himself, that Penny's reluctance to give her heart to the Lord stemmed from the fear that she might lose some of the chief's attention? Should she commit her life to God, she would then no longer be upon his conscience, and his interest in her might wane. Was she subconsciously afraid of that happening? Clyde wished he knew.

"Well, Penny, I'm glad of this break," Clyde spoke with feeling. "I haven't had a free long weekend since I left medical school.

Oh, yes, occasionally I have had an odd Saturday and Sunday off, but not three whole days." *And to spend it in your sweet company,* he added mentally, his eyes bright with anticipation.

"Do you like being on the wards?" Penny questioned, drawing another long breath of fresh air.

"It certainly is a change from Casualty."

"That new girl in orthopedics seems to have taken a fancy to you."

Clyde's face burned with embarrassment. "You mean Sylvia Blackwell, of course. But please don't think I've encouraged her in any way. I've been trying to help her — she's a difficult, mixed-up sort of a girl. You know what some of these teen-age girls are like — " He gestured and grinned. "It's so easy for a young girl to get a crush on a man, especially if the man in question happens to be a handsome, distinguished doctor like myself."

Involuntarily Penny giggled. Oh, it was good to be able to giggle freely, not having to stifle her natural exuberance, not having to tense herself against Michael's disapproving frown.

"Like me, you mean," There was a hint of mischief in her blue eyes. "Like my feelings for the handsome, distinguished Michael Ashmore."

"Perhaps." Clyde hesitated, then remarked eagerly: "At the end of the year I'm hoping to get my registrarship."

"Oh, that will be lovely, Clyde!" She gazed at him in frank delight.

"I shall then be able to afford a wife," he told her half playfully.

"Not Sylvia Blackwell, surely?"

He grinned. "No, not Sylvia Blackwell." Suddenly his face sobered and a tender expression crept into his eyes. "I have someone else in mind."

"Oh!" Penny could not understand her sudden sense of loss, as if her very best friend had let her down.

After a lengthy pause, she went on: "In a way I envy her, whoever she is. She's a fortunate girl."

Clyde was so different from Michael — not complex, but easy to understand. Sincere and sympathetic and yet so masculine, he would make a splendid husband, and Penny hoped that the girl would be worthy of him.

"When do you plan to be married?" Penny questioned with mingled curiosity and concern.

He grinned again. "I haven't asked her yet."

Penny wondered at her sense of relief.

Clyde continued: "She doesn't even know how I feel about her. But I intend to tell her at the end of the year, that is, if she hasn't got herself engaged to someone else by then. You see, there is another man."

Penny's gaze was full of sympathy. "So she's interested in someone else. Poor Clyde!" Gently she touched his sleeve. "I understand. Now we're both in the same position. You caring for this girl who is keen on someone else and I loving Michael, when he is so obviously wrapped up in Ruth."

Clyde halted abruptly. "What makes you say that? I haven't noticed anything special in the way he looks at her. As always, he treats her in the same cool manner."

"But with a subtle difference. I can tell — Michael can't fool me." Penny's lower lip began to tremble. "He's attracted to Ruth, that is obvious."

"You could be mistaken, you know." Clyde was frowning.

"I am not! A woman has an instinct about these things, you know. But I suppose I shouldn't really worry. You assured me Ruth wasn't at all keen on him, romantically, that is."

Clyde swallowed hard. He gazed down at his feet. He longed to tell Penny the truth, that he had since learned of Ruth's love for the superintendent. But the knowledge of this would doubtless cause the girl intolerable pain. She wasn't strong enough emotionally to hear the truth just yet. However, when she became a Christian, when she learned to put her trust in the Lord Jesus, then she would find in Him the solace to the ache in her heart.

If Penny was correct in her conjecture that Michael Ashmore was attracted to Ruth, Clyde could be glad for her sake, but certainly not at the expense of Penny's happiness. He wanted her happiness above all else.

Clyde was positive now that what his chief felt for Penny was only the affectionate regard of an older man toward a young girl whom he considered still a child. But what of Penny? Were her feelings for him those of a woman and not the adoration of a young girl for an older, distinguished man?

* * * * * * * *

In the hospital dining room the superintendent and Matron lingered over their coffee.

Dr. Ashmore glanced down at his watch. "My word," he ex-

110

claimed, "I'd no idea it was so late. Two o'clock already." He glanced across the table at Ruth. "So you're off this afternoon."

Her eyes did not mirror the smile which curved her lips.

"I shall be on duty again from five till eight," she told him, rising in her seat.

He followed suit. "Then I dare say you will want an early night."

"Not that early." She paused, wondering when he would come to the point. "I'm off for the day tomorrow. Leonora Radford has asked me to spend the day with her at Constantia, but seeing Penny is there with Clyde, I think I'll just go there for dinner after church tomorrow morning."

"H'm." Dr. Ashmore was stroking his chin reflectively. "Then how about having supper with me before going on to the evening service?"

Ruth nodded. "Thank you, Michael."

"Good." His eyes upon her were intent and oddly disconcerting. "Then what about tonight? Do you think you could manage to go out with me after you come off duty? I promise to bring you back early."

Ruth was conscious of her quickened pulse. She longed desperately to say yes. She yearned for his company, she wanted to be near him always. But there was Penny to consider — the girl Michael loved. Or did he? Ruth wasn't exactly sure now.

She had seen Penny in Michael's arms. He had held her close — very close. Michael was not a man who could love or display his affections easily. Everything pointed to his being in love with the younger girl — his anxiety over her spiritual welfare, his concern in the past lest she should become involved with Don Anderson.

Yet last Wednesday Dr. Ashmore had revealed genuine relief when he knew Penny would not be accompanying them to the meeting. Ruth recalled his exact words — "To tell the truth, I'd welcome a break from Penny tonight." These did not seem to be words of a man in love, but one could never be quite certain of Michael Ashmore's true feelings.

Then there had been his readiness to postpone their supper appointment to a time when Penny was not with them. That, too, was surely not the action of a man in love. Yet there had been his embrace — Ruth had witnessed it with her own eyes. If someone else had mentioned it to her, she would then perhaps not have believed it.

Matron and the superintendent were now walking along the side corridor. Automatically he stepped into pace beside her as they made their way across the grounds toward Ruth's flat which adjoined the nurses' quarters.

Outside the entrance to her flat they paused. Unexpectedly his hand came down on her arm in a gesture of entreaty.

"You haven't answered my question about tonight," he said softly.

She put a confused hand to her forehead. Her whole being responded to his nearness, his touch. She yearned to accept the invitation and yet — It was one thing to have supper with him and then together to go on to church. There would be others present. But to be alone with him tonight, perhaps driving along a lonely, winding country road or cruising slowly by the sea front, or up the mountainside to see the lights of the City —

It would be sheer folly, Ruth decided, to go out alone with him tonight. She was sure to give herself away. And that would never do.

Yet as she looked up into his gray eyes, eyes which at that moment seemed filled with some secret message, she was lost.

"All right," she whispered, "I'll come."

"Excellent!" He pressed her arm. "Till tonight then."

CHAPTER SEVENTEEN

At Ruth's suggestion Michael drove along the sea front in the direction of Clifton. Traffic was fairly heavy that way, and there seemed to be more people about. That was what Ruth wanted.

The sudden spell of fine weather was continuing. For the middle of July the air was not cold, just pleasantly bracing. It was a change from last week's cold snap. Two more months and it would be spring, then the southeasters would begin to blow.

For a while Matron and Doctor kept up a flow of conventional conversation. Then, suddenly, turning to her, he remarked:

"It was a relief when Penny eventually decided to accept Mrs. Radford's invitation to spend the weekend at Constantia. It will do the girl good to have Maxwell's companionship. I rather like him — he's a fine character."

Smiling, Ruth nodded. "Yes. I've always been fond of Clyde. He's a dear boy."

"His sister appears to be somewhat older."

"Leonora is the same age as I," Ruth responded, glancing at the passing traffic. "I think I've already mentioned to you that we're old school friends. Clyde was just a young boy when their parents died. I went in for nursing, but Leonora was forced to take up a more remunerative position. There was Clyde to support. Some money was left to them by their parents, but most of it was kept in trust for his medical school fees. Clyde wanted his sister to have the money, but she wouldn't hear of it — she was most keen for him to study medicine."

"And she didn't marry until quite recently," Michael put in, keeping his gaze on the road.

"That wasn't because she didn't have any proposals. Leonora

113

is a very attractive person. She didn't meet Mr. Right until she came across Colin Radford. But even then she hesitated to marry."

"You mean because of Robin?"

"Yes." Ruth nodded. "Now everything has worked out splendidly. The Lord has graciously answered prayer. Robin is a changed boy since he accepted Christ as his Saviour."

A small silence fell between Ruth and Michael.

Swinging the car to the right, he exclaimed: "My life has also been radically transformed. The Christian life is certainly worth living. Since my conversion I've proved this to be true time and time again. How on earth I existed before I came to know the Lord, I really don't know. Now my life has a new meaning. As the preacher said last Sunday, when one experiences the New Birth, it is like being created all over again. That is what has happened to me. I've become a new man, Ruth."

Wonderingly, Ruth turned to study the man at her side. Michael's eyes were glowing; his face had become alive, vital. Gone were the old hauteur, the cynicism, the cold reserve.

The doctor had now maneuvered his car into a parking bay overlooking the sea. Aware of her regard, he swung round to look at her. For a long, suspended moment they gazed at each other.

Was it her imagination, or were his eyes trying to convey to her some sort of message?

With determination she flicked her gaze away from his and hastily glanced at the restless Atlantic Ocean, not seeing the moonlight on the water or hearing the foamy waves crash against the cliffs. She was conscious only of the man at her side, of her own wildly thumping heart.

She should not have consented to come out with him this evening. The effort not to give herself away was proving a little too strong for her.

Michael was the first to shatter the long, eloquent silence. With apparent composure, he resumed: "It will be a great burden off my mind when Penny decides to commit her life to God. As you are well aware, she is very much on my heart and conscience. I feel responsible for her."

As she realized the implication of his words, a coldness entered Ruth's heart. Was Michael trying to tell her that he loved Penny? Ruth hoped that in the dim light her sudden pallor would escape observation.

Somehow Ruth managed to maintain her poise as she responded: "I'm praying earnestly that she will soon come to know the Lord. Have you made any progress with her?"

"Not much." Dr. Ashmore shook his head regretfully. "Penny has something on her mind. I wish she would confide in me. Perhaps you have some idea what it could be?"

Ruth sat silent, wondering what to say. She did not look at him. She felt his eyes peering anxiously at her, as he waited patiently for her answer.

"What about?" she countered with a question.

"I thought she may have confided in you. Perhaps I have not mentioned it, but I am Penny's legal guardian. I was her father's best friend and before Henry Fielding died, he asked me to take care of her. There was no one else he could ask or turn to except me. I promised faithfully I would do so. I had no idea what I would be taking on. Penny is quite a responsibility, I can tell you! And a problem," he ended with a wry smile.

Ruth didn't suppress her smile.

Before she could comment, the doctor continued: "That was why I was so concerned about her friendship with Anderson. Thank goodness that's all over now — it didn't come to anything! What a weight off my mind."

Ruth found the delirious joy of being in his company giving way to pain. His motive for seeking her out seemed quite obvious now. It was to discuss Penny — a not so subtle attempt to discover how she felt towards himself.

"It could be, of course," Michael's voice cut across Ruth's unhappy thoughts, "that she is still pining for Anderson. Yet somehow I have the impression that she has got over him."

His words compelled Ruth to let Dr. Ashmore know the truth.

"You are gravely mistaken, Michael. At no time has Penny ever been keen on Don Anderson. For a time she enjoyed his company — she found him gay and amusing, no doubt. But as regards any deeper feelings, I can assure you they positively didn't exist."

The doctor frowned in perplexity. "There appears to be some sort of misunderstanding. Penny was absolutely heartbroken when she heard of Anderson's engagement to Staff Gregory. I found her weeping unrestrainedly in my office. She was so forlorn, so dejected that I wouldn't have been human had I left her to weep on her own. After doing my utmost to console her,

I drove her home and spent part of the evening with her. When I left she seemed much brighter."

So that was the explanation! The explanation of the scene she had witnessed in Dr. Ashmore's office — the scene which had preyed on her mind for a whole fortnight.

"Now you see why you must be mistaken, Ruth."

She nodded, unable to still the hammering of her heart.

"So it seems," she murmured. Then added mentally: *But only where you are concerned, Michael dear.* Penny must have been weeping for quite a different reason. And it was not over the E.N.T. surgeon's engagement, of that Ruth was absolutely convinced.

"Ruth — " Michael's voice was unsteady, "I had a purpose in asking you out tonight."

"Yes?" Her voice was quite breathless.

"I wonder if you have ever considered marriage? I know so little of your past life," he confessed with a shy smile. "That is, your personal life. For my part, I admit that until recently marriage had not entered my head at all. Only now have I given it serious thought." The doctor paused. He seemed rather nervous, so unlike his calm, confident self.

She scarcely dared to glance at him for fear of betraying herself.

"The truth is I'd like to marry you, Ruth."

She could not speak. But her wonderfully expressive eyes told him all he wanted to know.

Suddenly he bent over her and kissed the lips raised so invitingly to his.

"Darling Ruth," he whispered huskily, "I love you."

Then he was kissing her again — kissing her with all the assurance of a man who knows the strength of his love and that his love is returned.

"Michael, my darling," she breathed in ecstasy, returning his kisses with equal fervor.

It was hard to believe that the man who was kissing her so ardently was really the dignified, austere medical superintendent of Oakhurst Hospital. It did not seem possible, somehow. Yet here she was, nestling in his arms and telling him how much she loved him.

When at last he released her, both were trembling from the unaccustomed emotion which had possessed them.

"Let's drive into Camps Bay for coffee," Michael suggested

when they had regained their composure. "There is so much we have to discuss and plan — our engagement, our marriage."

Across the coffee table, he reached out a hand to hers.

"How long," he asked, gazing intently into her eyes, "have you been aware of your love for me?"

Her mouth curved into a mischievous smile.

"For fourteen years," she whispered, her face warm and alive with love.

"Fourteen years!" He almost dropped her hand in surprise. "You must mean fourteen days or weeks, surely?"

"I mean fourteen years," she rejoined, still smiling at him.

"But that's incredible." He gazed at her in wonder. "I can scarcely believe it."

"Yet it's true all the same. Fourteen years ago I was twenty-one and proudly wearing my staff nurse's badge. You were about Clyde's age and doing your internship — a solemn, unsmiling young man, somewhat unsure of himself. You took your work very seriously, Michael, and I loved you for it."

"It's incredible," he repeated, staring hard at her. "And do you mean to say you've loved me all this time?"

She nodded. "Most definitely! I remember how heartbroken I was when you left to specialize. And when you returned some years later, you were the dignified consultant, remote and so — " she paused, "shall we say stern looking. Meanwhile I had achieved my ambition — I was a ward sister. But even then you scarcely deigned to glance at me. To tell the truth, I was a little afraid of you."

"What an insufferable, conceited snob I must have been."

"Oh, no, Michael," came her quick retort, "you were not a snob. You were so wrapped up in your work, in your patients. Even the poorest old lady would receive your meticulous attention. Your work came first at all times. I admired you for that and loved you for what you were. I love you more now," she added, affectionately pressing his hand. "Since you've become a Christian my love for you has deepened." Her face glowed with a soft light.

"It's astounding!" There was awe in his voice. "You amaze me. And I never knew, I never guessed. You never dropped a hint."

"Would it have made any difference if I had?" she asked him gently. "I guess not. Marriage was not included in your plans for a successful career. Your chief ambition was to become the medical superintendent."

117

"Yes, you're right." He nodded. Thoughtfully he sipped his coffee. "I achieved my ambition, yes. Yet I can't say it made me any happier. It gave me a certain satisfaction — and prestige. I was proud of what I had achieved. Yet there was an ache, a longing in my heart — a longing which only Christ could satisfy. Now He has not only given me His peace, His joy and satisfaction —" Michael's eyes were filled with love and tenderness, "but He has graciously given you to me. Though I became aware of my love only recently, I think I must have loved you from the time I started to study God's Word for Penny's sake. When shall we be married, Ruth?"

"For Penny's sake." Ruth murmured the words as if in a dream. Then a resolute gleam leaped into her eyes. "We can't do it, Michael. Not yet, anyway."

"What on earth are you talking about?"

"I'm afraid we'll have to wait a little longer before we can think of marriage."

"Wait?" The doctor sounded nonplused. "What on earth for? Neither of us is getting any younger. On Monday afternoon we'll see about the rings — wedding as well as engagement ring."

She smiled. "That will be lovely, darling." But the light had gone out of her eyes.

"What is the matter, my dearest?"

"Penny. I'm thinking of Penny. We'll have to consider her — there's no getting away from it."

"What on earth has she to do with our marriage?" he demanded, furrowing his brow in bewilderment.

"Everything. We just can't go ahead and be married without giving a thought to the effect it will have on her. We could become engaged, but please, Michael —" Ruth hesitated as she saw his heavy frown, "let it be a secret engagement for the time being."

"No!" His tone was firm, adamant. "Such nonsense I absolutely refuse to contemplate. It's utterly ridiculous. I insist on our engagement being made public. And that's final!"

Now he spoke as the superintendent of Oakhurst Hospital and not as the man who loved her.

"Michael —" Ruth's eyes pleaded with his. "Won't you give me a chance to explain?"

"Of course. Please forgive me, Ruth. What an autocrat I must sound."

"Penny is in love with you."

118

He smiled slowly. "That is no news. But I wouldn't call it love. It's a sort of doggy devotion — a hero-worship. Call it what you like. That shouldn't worry you, my darling."

"But it does worry me. Penny's love is not just something you can brush aside. We'll have to consider her reaction. At present she is in a highly emotional state. You say you found her weeping her heart out over Anderson's engagement to Phyl Gregory. But it was not her love for him which caused her such distress. It was the culmination of many things. For weeks Penny has been living in dread in case you should embrace the Christian faith, as she calls it." Ruth paused and looked steadily at the doctor. "This is no mere conjecture — no woman's intuition on my part."

"But how absurd."

"It may seem so to you. It's true all the same. She resented — and still does — my friendship with you. She was desperately afraid that should you become a believer, you would turn to me. She couldn't bear the thought of losing you."

Dr. Ashmore's frown deepened. "At no time has there ever been anything between Penny and me," he declared with emphasis. "You must believe me, Ruth."

She flashed him a reassuring smile. "Of course I believe you, Michael. I know you are fond of Penny — so am I — and that you have her welfare at heart. That is why we must keep our engagement secret for the time being."

"We'll do no such thing!" he stated firmly. "Our engagement may cause her some grief. But her weeping won't last. She'll soon learn to accept the true state of affairs. The young are very adaptable."

Ruth shook her head decisively. "It's no good, Michael — it's just no good. Penny is an insecure little person. There is her spiritual welfare to consider, and that is most important. Should she hear how things are between us, any good she may have received by attending church these past weeks may be completely nullified. Her faith in you and me — and in God — may be completely shattered. The risk is too great. She may do something dreadful. That's what I'm afraid of. Don't you see, my darling?" Ruth implored the doctor earnestly. "We can't risk announcing our engagement just yet."

His sigh was heavy with disappointment. "Yes, I suppose you're right. Penny has been on my conscience, I admit. But that's because of what happened some five years ago when I, by my heedless remarks, destroyed her faith in God. That text in Matthew 18:6 — 'Whoso shall offend one of these little ones which believe in Me' — has disturbed me for weeks — ever since that first Sunday I attended church with you."

"But God has forgiven you, Michael. So don't distress yourself any more over it."

Dr. Ashmore smiled. "I know He has. All the same, there are some things that require restitution. I'd do anything to undo the harm I unwittingly caused her. That is why I'm doing my utmost to help the girl spiritually. But she just won't yield. Something is holding her back."

"I may have the answer to that one," Ruth put in quietly. "Penny is afraid that once she commits her life to God, you may lose your interest in her. At present she is thoroughly reveling in your attentions — your spiritual concern."

"Couldn't you take her over, Ruth?" he asked her earnestly.

"It wouldn't do any good." She gestured significantly. "It's you she wants. But don't let's worry about the matter any more. Let's just leave our problem with the Lord. He will answer prayer in His own good time. Already I have waited fourteen long years for you. I can wait another fourteen years if necessary."

"Darling Ruth!" He leaned over the table and caught her hand in an affectionate grasp. "What have I done to deserve such faithfulness? The Lord has been very good in keeping you for me. An attractive woman like you could so easily have married years ago. I want right now to make you my wife. But as you say, we will have to wait. Bother Penny! If she'd only fall in love with someone else. Maxwell, for instance. He'd be ideal. A steady sort of fellow."

"I agree." Ruth nodded her brown head. "And in his own quiet way I should say he is more than a little fond of Penny."

"Well, then, that should solve our problem. She can marry Maxwell."

Ruth smiled. "Not quite. You forget Penny doesn't know the Lord."

"Hm. Then we're back where we started."

"It would seem like it. But nothing is too hard for the Lord. Let's return to the car and have a time of prayer," Ruth suggested, rising in her seat. "I've proved the Lord time and time again and I know He won't fail us now." And she smiled confidently at the man she loved so dearly.

CHAPTER EIGHTEEN

After the evening service there was a social in the church hall. When Clyde asked Penny whether she would like to remain, she nodded yes, not because she was at all eager to attend the social, but because she had seen Michael in church with Ruth. Now, still covertly watching them, Penny saw him take Ruth's arm as he escorted her toward the hall. Penny followed with Clyde, wishing fervently that Dr. Ashmore and not Clyde was her companion.

In spite of missing Michael so much, and constantly dreaming of him, she could in all honesty say that she was thoroughly enjoying her stay with Clyde's relatives at Constantia. They made her feel so completely at home. Clyde's sister was a dear, so considerate and kind, remarkably like him both in looks and character. She had refrained from asking any awkward or embarrassing questions, such questions as to whether she was Clyde's girl friend, did she intend to marry him or something equally absurd. Leonora accepted their friendship for what it was — purely platonic, and that was how Penny wanted it to remain.

Ruth had been present at Sunday dinner, a Ruth whose shining eyes and smiling lips caused both Penny and Leonora several times to glance speculatively at the matron. Her pale cheeks were tinged with color. There was about her an air of suppressed happiness, of excitement, as if something wonderful had happened or was about to happen to her.

After dinner, with a murmured "Excuse us," Ruth had disappeared with Clyde's sister in the study. Penny and Clyde had leisurely wandered out into the sunshine, Robin chatting gaily at Penny's side.

With a shrug she had dismissed Ruth from her mind, thinking

121

that it was hardly likely that Matron's happiness could in any way be related to Dr. Ashmore.

But now, observing Ruth and Michael together at the far side of the hall, noting the way they were smiling into each other's eyes, Penny struggled with her thoughts. She was strongly convinced that something strange was going on, and she determined to find out exactly what it was.

Her blue eyes gleaming with resolution, she approached Dr. Ashmore and Matron. At the sight of Penny, they stopped speaking abruptly, evidently not wishing her to overhear what they were saying.

"Hullo, Penny." Ruth was the first to greet her. "Glad to see you here tonight."

"Enjoying your weekend?" Michael put in pleasantly.

"Yes, thank you," she rejoined formally. Clyde was chatting to Ruth, so Penny took the opportunity to ask the doctor: "What's happened to you, Michael? You look different."

He made no comment. His eyes were guarded.

Penny was silent as she debated whether to voice her uneasy thoughts. Then she rushed into speech.

"You look younger and happier as if — " she floundered, "as if you could be in love."

Dr. Ashmore did not smile. He did not even try to laugh off the suggestion. Instead he frowned.

"I wish you'd mind your own business, Penny." His voice held cold rebuke.

She could not control her habit of blushing whenever he spoke sharply to her. Quickly she averted her eyes from the annoyance in his.

"I'm sorry." Here she was apologizing to him, as usual. Her eyes clouded with distress, with anxiety. She wished she had Ruth's smiling calm, Ruth who was so serene and poised always, whatever the turmoil of her thoughts.

"Michael — " She reached out a hand in a gesture of entreaty.

"That's all right," he said kindly. He patted her hand briefly, but his gaze was on Ruth.

Penny was relieved when Clyde returned to her side. She attempted a wan smile.

"Please take me home, Clyde." Her eyes implored him. He noted her effort not to betray her agitation.

"Anything wrong?" he inquired sympathetically.

She nodded. "I'll tell you in the car."

122

Mystified by her behavior, he took her arm and guided her through the crowd and out into the street. The air was bitterly cold. Penny shivered violently.

Without speaking, Clyde helped her into the car. There was a warm traveling rug on the back seat. This he took and draped round the quivering girl.

"Forgive me," Penny mumbled through chattering teeth, "for being such a nuisance."

"Now no more talking until we get back to the house," he told her in his best professional manner.

"But I want to go home," she protested weakly.

"I won't hear of it. You're staying at Constantia until tomorrow evening as arranged. Besides, Penny, you need someone to look after you. Leonora will help you."

"I'm not ill, Clyde. I can look after myself."

"No, you can't. I refuse to leave you alone in your present condition. You'd only brood and that won't help you."

"I've had a shock. That's why I'm shaking so."

He smiled gently at her before starting up the car. "Like to tell me about it?"

"Oh, Clyde!" she burst out in a tearful voice. "It's Michael and Ruth. There is something between them — I know there is! To-night I could sense it. Please don't tell me I'm imagining things, because I'm not."

The intern looked grave. "I wouldn't dare suggest it. Yes," he admitted, "I could also sense something."

The way Matron and the Chief had looked at each other! There was a wealth of meaning in their exchanged glances.

"Oh, dear!" A low moan escaped Penny's lips. "Do you think they're engaged — perhaps planning to be married?"

"I wouldn't know." He gave a helpless shrug. "I'm as much in the dark as you are, Penny."

"But didn't Ruth say anything to you when you were talking?" Penny gazed at him, her eyes filled with anguish.

"We were discussing Robin." He and Leonora had attended the evening service at their own church.

Clyde extended a compassionate hand. Almost desperately Penny clasped his, as if reaching out toward his strength and calmness.

"Oh, Clyde, what would I do without you?"

He was silent. He yearned to take her in his arms, to console her in a more personal way. But most of all, he prayed that in

123

simple faith she would learn to lean upon the Lord who was the source of all true comfort. In Him she would find her peace, her joy.

When they arrived at the Radford home, Leonora and Robin had not yet returned from church. Most likely, Clyde told Penny, they had gone visiting after the service. As Mr. Radford was away, Leonora was using her husband's car, having offered her own to her brother to take Penny to church.

A Bantu servant was hovering around, wanting to know whether he should serve tea. Thanking him, Clyde led Penny into the lounge. He switched on the electric fire. She seated herself, took off her gloves and began to rub vigorously her stiff, cold hands.

"The cup that cheers." Smiling, Clyde handed her a steaming cup of tea. "This should warm you."

"Thanks." Gratefully she accepted the tea. *Clyde is really a dear,* she mused.

Suddenly she smiled at him. "What a nuisance I am! I dare say you must think me something of a fool."

"Not at all," he replied gravely. "I can understand how you feel, Penny."

"That's because you care for this girl who is fond of someone else." Thoughtfully she sipped her tea. She could not understand any girl not failing to appreciate Clyde. She herself was growing quite fond of him.

"Do you feel jealous? I do." She had been shocked by the feelings of jealousy aroused by the sight of Michael and Ruth so obviously enjoying each other's company.

"Can't say I do," Clyde rejoined. "Her happiness means much to me."

"Oh, Clyde," she broke in miserably, "do you think that Michael and Ruth will make a match of it? If they do it will mean the end of me. I'll have no incentive to go on living."

"Now you're talking sheer nonsense." She looked so pathetic, so defenseless and griefstricken that Clyde's heart smote him. "You're young, Penny, young and pretty. There are other men besides the chief, you know. In my opinion Dr. Ashmore is too old for you."

"Don't say that!" she cried vehemently. "Age doesn't matter in love."

"Perhaps not in all cases. But in this one it does." Clyde paused. "Now that the chief is a believer, have you given a thought to accepting the Lord for yourself? Dr. Ashmore will be pleased, I know."

"But I'm not an unbeliever. Not any longer."

Joy leaped into Clyde's heart. "Do you mean that, Penny? You really believe in God — you have put your trust in the Lord?"

Penny's blue eyes were slightly defiant. "Well, not exactly. But I'm no longer an agnostic. I do believe in God."

"Wonderful! I'm so happy to hear it. If you accept Christ as your Saviour, if you put your faith and trust in Him, you will discover He is more than willing to meet your need. The Lord will become all-important to you, far more important than Dr. Ashmore is at present."

"Michael will always come first with me." Her lips set obstinately.

"Not if you love the Lord," Clyde intervened with a smile.

"Oh, Clyde!" Penny ejaculated in a tearful voice. "I'm so miserable. Michael and I were getting along splendidly before Ruth came on the scene. Now she has spoiled everything for me. I have no chance against her."

"You seem to have forgotten that Ruth has known the chief for fourteen years," Clyde reminded Penny gently. "So it's not a case of Ruth coming on the scene. Besides, there was no understanding between you and the chief. There never has been. So your accusations are quite unjustified."

"Now you're taking Ruth's part," Penny pouted rebelliously.

Clyde was silent. Then he observed: "We don't know for sure that there's anything between them. Let's wait and see, shall we, before jumping to conclusions. Here, let me pour you another cup of tea."

On Tuesday morning Penny acknowledged the superintendent's cheerful greeting without her usual smile. But Dr. Ashmore appeared not to notice that anything was amiss.

"Hope you enjoyed your long weekend."

"I did." She spoke a little defiantly, her gaze on the filing cabinet.

"Maxwell is a good lad," the doctor went on pleasantly. "He should go far in the profession. He has the makings of an excellent doctor."

"Michael — ?" Her voice held a question.

The doctor glanced up from his diary. "I see I'm due this morning at a medical conference. I shall have to leave right away if I want to be on time. See you later, Penny." He paused in the doorway. "I shall phone you as usual to find out if there are any important messages. If anything urgent should come through, please don't hesitate to phone me. You'll find the number in the diary."

"Very good, Doctor," she replied formally.

He darted her a quick look before leaving the office.

The intercom buzzed. It was Matron wanting to speak to Dr. Ashmore. Then next instant: "It's all right, Penny. Doctor has just walked in."

So Michael had gone to say good-by to Ruth. No wonder he was in such a hurry to leave. Again Penny felt the pangs of jealousy.

June, July and August, the winter months, were busy ones at the hospital. As the superintendent's secretary, Penny was kept fully occupied. There was little time for reflection.

Some nights she would lie awake, unable to sleep, her mind torn by conflicting emotions as she dwelt on Michael and Ruth. Unsuccessfully she tried to analyze their every look, their gestures, their speech. Apparently there was a slight cooling off on either side, and this made Penny glad. Ruth did not come into Dr. Ashmore's office except when absolutely necessary. And the same could be said of him. These days he invariably spoke to Matron over the intercom and their conversation was purely professional.

Of course they would see each other in church. But that, Penny decided, was unavoidable. Penny still accompanied the doctor to church; she would not for anything give up that pleasure. Besides, she was beginning to derive some enjoyment from the services themselves. She willingly joined in the singing of well-known hymns; she even found herself listening intently to what the preacher had to say. And she was always delighted to meet Clyde. These days she did not often encounter him at the hospital. Most of the intern's time was spent on the wards, occasionally assisting in theater.

Soon it was spring. The September sunshine was warm and inviting. New grass was appearing, buds were proudly unfolding their beauty; the oaks stood in splendid new dress. On some days the southeasters would mercilessly whip the trees, then the next day the wind would relent and peace would reign for a few more days.

The week that Penny was on duty on Saturday morning, she was given Wednesday afternoon off. This afternoon she decided to take a trip into Cape Town, have lunch and afterwards do some shopping. She intended to buy herself a new spring outfit.

At 12:30 sharp Dr. Ashmore left his office to have an early lunch. She naturally concluded he was lunching as usual in the staff dining room. She was therefore astounded to see him in town with Ruth van Rhyn. They were standing close together outside the window of an exclusive jeweler. Her hand rested confidently on his arm. Their gaze was focused on a tray of engagement rings.

Her face blanching with apprehension, Penny stood and watched as if in a trance. Then the doctor's authoritative voice reached her ears and his words began to thrust themselves through to her consciousness.

"I absolutely refuse to keep up this pretense any longer, even for the sake of Penny. I'm determined that our engagement shall be announced this evening. Now let's go inside to choose your ring . . ." His voice trailed away.

Unable to think coherently, her body numb with mental anguish, Penny could only stand and stare. Passersby jostled her, but she paid no heed.

Then because she did not want to be seen by Doctor and Matron when they came out of the jeweler's, she began to walk down the street as swiftly as her shaking limbs would permit. Somehow she managed to hold in her hurt until she reached her car.

Still in a daze, she climbed into the driver's seat and folding her arms on the steering wheel, she buried her aching head on them. Next moment she gave vent to a storm of bitter, passionate tears.

CHAPTER NINETEEN

As Penny was not on duty on Wednesday afternoon, she was not missed by the superintendent. When, however, she failed the next day to put in an appearance at the hospital, Dr. Ashmore began to wonder if she had heard of his engagement to Ruth van Rhyn. Perhaps Penny was genuinely ill. But then surely she would have telephoned him or asked her housekeeper to contact the hospital.

Shortly after morning tea the telephone rang in Matron's office. Proudly wearing a sparkling engagement ring, Ruth lifted the receiver. Penny's voice, sounding strangely different, came over the line.

"How are you, Penny?"

"I'm fine." Her young voice held a hard edge.

"That's good. Dr. Ashmore will be relieved to know you're all right. Shall I ask the exchange to put you through to him?"

"Don't bother. I don't want to speak to Doctor. It's you I wish to talk to, Ruth."

A cold feeling of premonition clutched at her heart.

"Couldn't you come and see me here?"

"No. I shall not be returning to Oakhurst."

"But you can't let Doctor down like this," Ruth protested.

"I can! And I will!" Penny spoke resolutely. "You seem to forget how badly he has let me down."

"That's not true. You've got it all wrong, Penny."

"Have I? I hardly think so." There was a long pause. Then: "Doctor can quite easily get a secretary from one of the secretarial services. He would have to do so in any case if I were ill. You can tell Doctor that."

128

"Very well, if that's what you want. I'm sorry that you should feel this way."

"But you're not sorry that you have taken Michael away from me. You regret only my reaction."

"I know how you must feel, Penny. I'm deeply sorry. I only wish you would get your facts straight, then you would see things differently. I strongly repudiate your statement that I have taken Dr. Ashmore away from you."

"Then what do you call it?" Penny asked truculently.

"Listen, Penny," said Ruth patiently. "I'd rather we didn't continue this discussion over the telephone. Won't you come here so that we can talk things over?".

"No! I will not!"

"Then may I call on you? I'm off duty this afternoon between two and five p.m."

"All right," Penny agreed after a lengthy pause.

Ruth was replacing the receiver when the superintendent walked into the office.

"That another congratulation?" he inquired with a tender smile.

"No." She shook her head gravely. "That was Penny on the line. She's not coming back, Michael."

The smile left his face. "Good grief! I didn't think she'd take it as badly as all that."

"I'm going to see her this afternoon. I'll try to talk some sense into her."

"Hm." The doctor sat down and reflectively stroked his chin. "These many weeks I've done my utmost to help the girl, to lead her to the Lord. I neglected you in order to spend most of my time with her. But she's obstinate — she absolutely refuses to yield. That state of affairs couldn't continue any longer, you realize that. It's you I love and want to marry. I should have told Penny outright instead of agreeing to keep our love a secret for her sake. It was bound to come out eventually."

"Perhaps we should have left it that way — we should have continued to keep it a secret . . . . " And Ruth shrugged helplessly.

"Nonsense! I disagree there. I refuse to be dictated to by some slip of a girl. Years ago I unwittingly harmed Penny spiritually. This I bitterly regret. But, as you yourself have reminded me so many times, the Lord has forgiven me. He knows I have tried to make restitution by doing my best to restore her faith in Him. I've given in to many of her whims and fancies, but I refuse to allow her to dictate my love life." The doctor paused.

His steel-gray eyes regarded earnestly the woman he loved. "Pity I'm not free to accompany you this afternoon. I'm due in theater at 2:30."

"I can manage Penny." Ruth smiled at him.

"Perhaps." He returned her smile. "But not when she starts pleading with you to give me up."

"That I will never do. I promise you, Michael."

"Good." He looked considerably relieved. "Even should she promise to become a Christian if you broke it off with me, don't listen to her."

"I won't. So you can rest assured." She flashed him an affectionate smile.

"But you don't know Penny. She's a most determined young lady."

"Don't I know it!" Ruth grimaced. "Come on, Michael, relax. Let's have a word of prayer together." Gently she reached out a hand to his.

From the window Penny saw Ruth alight from her car. She had discarded her matron's blue uniform and headveil. Dressed in a smart spring suit, the sunlight playing upon her smooth brown head, Ruth made a pleasing and attractive picture, Penny had to admit. She did not in any way appear old or dowdy. No one could deny or dispute that she was a fitting fiancée for the meticulous Dr. Ashmore.

Firmly repressing her emotions, Penny went out onto the veranda to meet her. At once Ruth was struck by the other's pallor, the dark smudges beneath the blue eyes. Her heart went out in sympathy to the grief-stricken girl.

Ruth suggested they sit out on the veranda where they could enjoy both the sunshine and the garden, which on this lovely spring afternoon looked its best with gay flowers fringing the lawns.

They sat down opposite each other. Peace and tranquility lay everywhere, except in Penny's heart. Today the sunshine held no appeal for her. It might as well have been pouring with rain for all she cared.

She couldn't prevent herself from gazing down at Ruth's left hand and seeing the gorgeous diamond engagement ring she was wearing. Involuntarily tears stung Penny's eyes.

Tentatively Ruth put out a hand in a gesture of sympathy. Almost fiercely the younger girl brushed aside the extended hand.

"There's no need for you to sympathize. You're not at all sorry,

130

otherwise you wouldn't have got engaged to him. After repeatedly denying that there was anything between you and Doctor, you have deliberately stolen from me the man I love."

Ruth was quiet for so long that Penny rushed into speech again.

"And don't you try to deny it. Remember that time — it must be about five months ago now, that you asked me into your office?"

Ruth nodded wordlessly.

"You solemnly assured me then that there was absolutely nothing between you and Doctor, that your interest in him was purely spiritual. You wanted to help him to find the Lord. You led me to believe that Doctor was attending church mainly because of me — he was trying to discover the truth for himself in order to help me."

"That is quite correct," Ruth pointed out quietly.

"H'm!" Penny sniffed scornfully. "You deliberately and callously deceived me."

"That I strongly deny. At the time Dr. Ashmore had no romantic interest in me whatsoever."

"If that was the case, why didn't you leave him alone?" Penny demanded angrily. "You knew how I felt about him, yet you deliberately encouraged him."

Ruth sighed patiently. "I can see it's useless to continue this conversation. If you refuse to believe the truth, there is nothing further for me to say." Calmly she rose to her feet.

"Please don't go." No longer could Penny contain herself. "Oh, Ruth, I'm so miserable! So utterly wretched. What am I to believe?" Her face was piteous.

"Listen, Penny." Ruth's tone was firm yet kind. "For your own peace of mind you must believe that I'm speaking the truth."

"What if I believe you? It can make no difference now." Penny gestured in despair. "Michael is lost to me for good. He has fallen in love with you."

Ruth said gently: "It's a great mistake to pin all your hope and trust in one person, to make him into a kind of god. For years you have idolized Michael. That sort of adoration is not healthy, you know. In His Word God declares that we should worship no other god except Him. He alone is completely worthy of our adoration and faith."

"Now don't try to justify yourself." Penny looked at Ruth and saw the sincerity in her expression. "All right — I admit I did worship Michael. That is all finished now. But that doesn't mean

I want to lose him to you. Michael is still necessary to me. I need him desperately, Ruth. He is the only one who really matters to me." She paused, took a deep breath and continued: "Isn't there anything you can do or say to make him turn to me? You have your career — you have lived without Doctor for so long. It would be less of a loss to you — "

"I happen to love Michael very much. And he loves me. I couldn't contemplate giving him up. And quite frankly, I doubt whether he'd be pleased with the idea."

"How soon do you plan to marry?" Penny questioned with a sigh.

"We haven't fixed a date yet."

Penny considered for a moment. "I've made arrangements to go away for a long holiday. Ruth — " beseechingly she gazed at the older girl. "Won't you give me a promise? Without hope of any sort I couldn't go on living."

Penny was not one to admit defeat, Ruth realized.

"What do you want me to promise?" she asked, drawing a sharp breath.

"That you will not go ahead with any plans to be married until you hear from me. During the time I'm away I'm hoping Michael will miss me so much that he would do anything to get me to come back." Penny's smile was wry. "But I don't suppose there's any likelihood of that." She sighed wearily. "I didn't sleep a wink last night."

"But you feel happier now?"

She nodded. "A little. I do believe you have told me the truth, Ruth."

The older girl offered up a prayer of praise and thankfulness.

"Now, about that promise, Ruth."

"How long do you propose to be away?"

Penny shrugged. "That depends. Maybe six months, maybe a year. I can't say."

Ruth pursed her lips thoughtfully. "You're asking me to promise something which is going to prove very difficult." She paused. "Where do you intend going?"

Penny swung her slim legs. "That will be a secret. I'm not telling. But I shall contact you now and again to find out whether Michael is missing me and wants me back. I know I can rely on you to tell me the truth." Impulsively Penny caught hold of Ruth's hand.

"Thank you." Her voice shook with relief. "Now it's your turn to promise me something." She pulled a New Testament from her handbag. "I want you to promise that you will faithfully read a few verses from God's Word every day. This Book holds the key to all your problems. It can help you to sort out your mixed-up emotions. Give the Lord a chance to speak to you, Penny. Please! Only He can give you the security that you so badly need."

"All right." Frowning, Penny took the New Testament, though not unwillingly. "It's a promise, Ruth. Now let's have a cup of tea. I'm absolutely parched."

CHAPTER TWENTY

"Phew! What a morning," exclaimed Dr. Maxwell, pausing at Matron's table in the staff dining room. "Two delicate brain operations in one morning. To assist at one is enough for me."

Ruth gestured to the intern to sit down. She studied him closely, noting Clyde's unusual pallor, the marks of strain on his face.

"What about the chief? Won't he be joining you?"

"Dr. Ashmore is attending a medical luncheon. Tell me, how did the operations go? Were they successful?"

A waitress approached the intern. He ordered steamed fish; then, turning to Ruth, he said: "The first one was a complete success. But the other —" he shook his head doubtfully. "Only time will tell. It was one of those ghastly accidents again. A motorcyclist without a crash helmet."

Ruth nodded regretfully. "That was the boy who was admitted late last night, or rather early this morning. What was he doing speeding around long after midnight? Sheer neglect on the parents' part. They've confessed as much."

The waitress brought Clyde his order. He bowed his head in thanksgiving. He ate slowly, without relish, as if he had lost his appetite.

"Anything on your mind, Clyde?" She leaned forward in concern.

He glanced up smiling. "I'm all right. Just a little tired and in need of a holiday. It's been a busy year for me." He sighed. "And now it's all over. When I return from my holiday it will be as medical registrar. I'm looking forward tremendously to going away next week. Jolly decent of Colin to offer me the loan of his house at Leisure Isle. It's situated right on the

Knysna Lagoon. He's even offered me the loan of his power boat. He knows I'm keen on boating."

Ruth smiled fondly. "You deserve a break, Clyde. You've worked very hard this year. Will you be away for the whole of December?"

He shook his head, his eyes still sad. "I intend to be back for Christmas. Leonora and Colin have asked me to spend it with them. Then on Boxing Day they'll be driving down to Leisure Isle to enjoy a little holiday. Of course Robin will be going with them."

"How is the new car?" Ruth asked, wishing she knew what was troubling Clyde.

His somber eyes lit up. "I'm most pleased with it." He paused, growing suddenly embarrassed. "If you should hear from — Penny — while I'm away, I'd be glad if you'd let me know, Ruth. Truth is, I'm rather anxious to hear how she's getting on."

"I most certainly will. She's been gone about two months and not a word from her. She said she'd contact me, yet there's been no card or telephone call. Wonder what's keeping her from getting in touch? She promised she would." Ruth's serene eyes were perplexed. "Doctor is becoming somewhat impatient. He'd like to take his leave at the end of January — we're thinking of getting married then. But what's the use of planning anything without first hearing from Penny?" And Ruth shook her head significantly.

Two months ago when Ruth had returned from her visit to Penny, Dr. Ashmore had been considerably displeased to learn that his fiancée had conceded to the girl's absurd request.

"It's ridiculous! Penny had no right to extract such a promise from you. Please phone her at once and tell her from me that she's being utterly foolish. I love you and intend to marry you as soon as everything can be arranged."

"But, Michael — "

He silenced her protest with a kiss. "Please phone her right away and tell her from me — "

Ruth moved away from his arms. "I can't do it, Michael. If you had seen her — she looked so desolate, so completely bewildered. The poor child is living in the hopes that you will miss her — "

"Of course I miss her! She's a bright, efficient secretary. Before she came obsessed with this fear of hers — that I'd fall in love with you — she was a delightful little person."

135

"Now her fears have been confirmed," Ruth put in with a sigh, half of contentment, half of regret. "It's a pity that out of our happiness so much sorrow has come. Poor sweet little Penny!"

"Her emotions are entirely misplaced. I'm not worthy of such adoration, such doglike devotion."

Ruth smiled affectionately at him. "I can't understand any girl or woman not admiring you."

Tenderly he smiled back. "As long as you admire me that's all that matters. I want and need only your love, dearest Ruth."

As the weeks passed they anxiously awaited news of Penny. But none came. That morning, before setting off to attend the medical luncheon, Dr. Ashmore had made his usual inquiry: "Still no news?" Then, as his fiancée regretfully shook her head, he gave an exasperated sigh. "Really! Most inconsiderate of her. She could at least have dropped us a line. What game does she think she's playing? I've a good mind to hire a private investigator."

Clyde's voice jerked Ruth back to the present moment.

"Wonder what's keeping her from writing or phoning? Anything could have happened to her. Perhaps she is ill — perhaps she is laid up in a hospital somewhere . . . ." Ruth heard the despair in his voice.

"Don't worry, Clyde. I'm sure Penny is all right. If she's been admitted to a hospital, the authorities would have contacted Dr. Ashmore."

"But she may be alone in some upcountry hotel desperately in need of help." His good-natured face registered his inward suffering.

"You're fond of Penny, aren't you?"

He nodded without speaking.

Ruth was also silent. She had guessed Clyde's feelings for the girl, but not for a moment had she imagined they went quite so deeply. Small wonder that her disappearance was causing him such anguish of spirit. Yet these past few weeks he had carried out his duties at the hospital with his usual cheerful smile, composed and apparently untroubled.

Clyde had planned to leave for Knysna at six o'clock on Monday morning. He wanted to reach the famous lakeside country town before nightfall. As his car was still new, he did not intend to travel at too great a speed. He would then enjoy the beauty of the Garden Route; his jaded mind and spirit would draw refreshment and strength from the glories of God's handiwork.

CHAPTER TWENTY-ONE

From the window of her little log-built bungalow, Penny had a view of the sea through the famous Knysna Heads, those great rocks which stood like sentinels guarding the entrance to the lagoon.

After their restless tossing last night, the sea and lagoon lay silent in the early morning sunshine. Gentle waves washed over the warm sand, while small children laughed in ecstasy, reveling in the glory of a new summer's day.

Her blue eyes contemplative, clasped hands resting lightly upon her head, Penny stood for a long while lost in reverie.

It was all so peaceful, so delightful. She did not want to leave Knysna; she did not want to return to the hospital, did not want to see Dr. Ashmore ever again. Something had died within her the day she had seen him with Ruth van Rhyn outside the jeweler's, when she had heard him speak those revealing words. For fear of hurting her, he and Ruth had kept their love a secret. They had not tried to deceive her; there had never been any understanding between Dr. Ashmore and herself. It had been a case of wishful thinking on her part. She could blame only herself for the disillusionment she had suffered.

By the twenty-third of the month she had to vacate the bungalow. New tenants were moving in for Christmas and New Year. Just three weeks were left for her to enjoy the splendor of the sea and lagoon, the grandeur of the countryside.

She remembered the day she had arrived at the Knysna Heads, tense and strung up and bitterly disillusioned, her mind torn with conflicting emotions.

No longer were her thoughts confused; there was no conflict in her mind. No longer were her emotions sadly misplaced. At long last she could see things in their proper perspective.

137

In her desperate search for security and her longing for love, she had reached out to Michael, hoping to find in him the emotional fulfillment she craved. But she had found neither security nor love. She realized with a pang that the doctor could give her none of these things. He was powerless to satisfy the ache in her heart.

Shamelessly she had thrown herself at Dr. Ashmore. She alone was to blame for her folly. The doctor had no romantic interest in her whatsoever. At no time had he ever encouraged her in her foolish dreaming. He had never given her any cause to dream or hope.

What a nuisance I must have been! Her cheeks burned with humiliation at the memory.

Opening the window wide, she let out a deep sigh, as if expelling from her mind all her past bewilderment, her misery and tension. Now, at last, she knew peace and satisfaction; she, who for so long had resisted God's Holy Spirit, had now received the Lord Jesus Christ as her own Saviour.

Last night the miracle had happened. Since her arrival at Knysna, she had faithfully read a few verses of Scripture every evening before retiring. She could not explain why it was that the reading of God's Word should give her a feeling of security. But because it did, she continued with her reading. It helped her to fall asleep in a more relaxed frame of mind.

She was thankful now that she had done so, for last night had been the turning point in her life. She had found the Lord! Through the reading of the precious words in John 14:6 — "I am the Way, the Truth and the Life, no man cometh unto the Father but by Me" — she had come to know the One who had died for her sins. She had committed her life to God and she had received His forgiveness. She was now a new person in Christ.

Far too long she had been in bondage; too long her mind and spirit had been dominated by Michael Ashmore.

This glorious feeling of freedom pulsated through her whole being. She had not thought she would ever feel happy again. Yet here she was feeling happier than she could ever recall. And without Michael!

She should really get in touch with Ruth, who no doubt was anxiously waiting to hear from her so that she and Michael could go ahead with their wedding plans.

At first she had been reluctant to phone Ruth. She dreaded to hear that Michael did not want her back, that he did not need her, that he had not missed her as much as she fervently hoped he would.

Strange, but after her first few days at Knysna, she herself had not missed him fully as much as she had expected. Gradually nature had done its healing work; Michael's face was becoming a blur. Instead she was seeing another face — a serious, sensitive face with gentle brown eyes. She longed suddenly to share her new-found freedom, her joy with Clyde, longed that he should know that she now belonged to the Lord.

Standing on tiptoe, she stretched her arms above her head.

"I'm free!" she whispered exultantly. "Free. Free of a dream!"

This afternoon she decided to drive up to town. It was high time she sent a telegram to Ruth. Meanwhile she would make the most of this glorious morning by taking a long walk to Leisure Isle. It had been some days since she had walked that way.

Putting on her sunglasses and walking sandals, she went gaily down the steps and out into the sunshine. She inhaled deeply, appreciating the soft, sweet air.

On the opposite side of the lagoon, gently curving hills rose out of the water, mirroring themselves in the smooth, sparkling surface. It was all so peaceful, so soothing, an ideal spot for taut, tired nerves to unwind.

As she strolled leisurely along the road bordering the lagoon, she saw several power boats moored at the water's edge. One young man, dressed in a gay sports shirt, was about to step into a boat named "Sally." There was something vaguely familiar in the shape of his brown head, the sturdy shoulders —

He turned briefly.

"Clyde!" she ejaculated in delight. Her heart gave a little lurch that was as surprising as it was sweet. Her blue eyes peered into his face in wonder, as if she were seeing him for the very first time.

"Penny! Is it really you?" His mouth curved in a warm smile.

He could scarcely credit the evidence of his eyes. Here before him stood the girl who lately had dwelt constantly in his thoughts, the girl for whom he had been praying so ardently since the day he had met her in the hospital corridor, hugging a bunch of white carnations.

Deliberately he searched her face. The animation in her eyes, the healthy glow on her cheeks presented to him a picture of a different Penny from the girl who had left her employment at the

139

hospital so precipitously. The marks of strain were gone from her face. No longer was she tense and despairing, imprisoned in her dream world into which he could not enter.

"So this is where you've been hiding yourself," Clyde grinned cheerfully.

"And what are you doing here at Leisure Isle?"

"This is my holiday. But come aboard and let's have a talk." He held her hand as she stepped happily into the boat. "Sit down and tell me all about yourself," he invited.

Penny shook her chestnut head. "You first. Mine is rather a long story. Where are you staying?" she asked eagerly.

"At my brother-in-law's house. There's the house just behind us." Clyde gestured. "The boat is his as well."

"Do you do your own cooking?" she asked with a mischievous smile.

He grinned. "No fear! There's a couple in charge of the place, but mostly I have my meals at the hotel. The family will be coming down after Christmas. I'm planning to return on the twenty-third."

Penny was conscious of her quickened pulse. "What a coincidence. So am I. I have to get out by then — my landlady tells me my bungalow has been rented by a couple coming to stay over the Season. I'm staying at the Knysna Heads — I have my meals in the restaurant," she added. "Sometimes I cook my own lunch. At first I thought of coming to stay here at the hotel, but I love the view of the sea from my window. Yesterday we had a strong southeaster — it was too windy for walking, so I just sat at the window watching the waves crash against the rocks. I find it stimulating, yet so restful and relaxing to live close to nature."

"So do I." He nodded thoughtfully. "You've changed, Penny. Something has happened to you."

"You're right! Something wonderful has happened to me." Her voice broke with deep emotion. "Last night I came to know the Lord as my Saviour. I was reading the New Testament — Ruth gave me a copy when she came to see me at home. I promised I'd read it. At first I began reading God's Word merely out of obligation, but then I found I was becoming really interested. The Scriptures had something to offer me. The Words of the Lord — 'I am the Way, the Truth and the Life, no man cometh unto the Father but by Me' — these words struck me forcibly. I felt compelled to yield — I couldn't resist God's Spirit any

140

longer. I'm glad now that I did," she finished, her blue eyes sparkling with joy.

Impulsively he caught her hand. "Oh, Penny! I'm so thankful. We must praise and thank the Lord for answer to prayer. Several people have been praying so earnestly for you. Have you phoned Ruth to let her know?"

"I was going to send her a telegram this afternoon."

"She'll be absolutely overjoyed. And the chief as well."

"They're not married yet?"

"No. They're patiently waiting to hear from you."

Penny's face flushed with embarrassment. "Apparently you know about that absurd promise I extracted from Ruth. What a silly donkey I've been!"

Relief was reflected in Clyde's face. "So you don't love the chief any more?"

Penny's smile was without a trace of bitterness.

"I'm free of a dream. It was wonderful while it lasted, but oh, so painful."

"Let's celebrate," Clyde suggested shyly. His eyes were tender behind his sunglasses. "Let's have lunch together at the hotel. Then tomorrow — "

She held her breath. "Yes . . . . "

"Tomorrow we'll take a trip up the lake. Maybe we'll go as far as the Wilderness."

"That would be lovely! But couldn't we rather go out to sea?"

"Well — " He looked doubtful. "I'm not experienced enough to take the boat out to sea. Perhaps if the weather holds and a southeaster doesn't spring up, we might chance it. Now, about that telegram — Better still, we'll phone them. I suggest we don't keep Ruth and the chief waiting a moment longer than necessary."

* * * * * * * *

Ruth smoothed down her blue uniform, picked up the reports from her desk and walked briskly along the hospital corridor in the direction of the superintendent's office.

Before entering, she stood for a moment on the threshold looking in and thought how tired and strained Michael was. His head was bent over some papers on his desk. There was a suggestion of despair in the sag of the slim shoulders.

Becoming aware of his fiancée, Dr. Ashmore glanced up and

smiled affectionately — a smile that erased some of the tiredness from his face.

"Come inside and close the door. Haven't seen much of you today." He paused before voicing his usual question. "Any news?"

Ruth shook her head and sat down.

The doctor's lips set in a determined line. "I refuse to wait any longer, Ruth. It's high time something was done about contacting Penny. At this rate we'll be waiting forever. My leave is fixed for the end of January. I know there's still plenty of time, but I like arrangements to be made well in advance."

The telephone on his desk shrilled loudly. Frowning at the interruption, the superintendent picked up the receiver.

"For you, Ruth. It's Clyde on the line." Dr. Ashmore handed her the receiver.

Ruth listened in silence. Watching her intently, the doctor saw relief and joy sweep into her face. When at last she replaced the receiver, she could scarcely speak for the deep emotion which shook her.

"Michael — it's all so wonderful!" Ruth breathed, her eyes shining with unshed tears. "I can scarcely believe it even now. Penny has been found. She and Clyde met by accident at the Knysna lagoon. Penny's been staying at the Heads all these weeks and we didn't know it."

Ruth paused for breath. The doctor placed a tender hand on her shoulder.

Swallowing hard, she continued: "But the most wonderful part is this: Penny has been faithfully reading the New Testament I gave her, and is now a believer." Again Ruth paused. "A few days ago the Lord gave me this promise in Ruth 3:18 — 'Sit still, my daughter, until thou know how the matter will fall.' I'm glad now that I made that promise to Penny. It's been worth the long wait. Oh, Michael, I'm so happy!"

He held her close. "At last," he murmured, in a strangely husky voice. "God has answered prayer. The Lord truly is wonderful. And here was I beginning to doubt. I'll never doubt again, I promise you."

142

CHAPTER TWENTY-TWO

The next day dawned — a clear, warm day; not a cloud was to be seen in the bright blue sky.

A whisper of a breeze caressed the surface of the lagoon, which shimmered under the low, rolling hillside.

Through the Heads, Penny caught a glimpse of the sea. How inviting it looked, with the sun shining on the gently rippling surface.

When she met Clyde as arranged, he told her that last night he had telephoned his brother-in-law just to make sure it would be all right to take "Sally" out to sea.

"As long as the weather is fine and there is no wind," Colin had assured him.

"Well, we couldn't have a more perfect day," Clyde added, smiling happily at Penny.

"How thrilling!" In sheer delight she clasped her hands. "A trip in a power boat. It's been my ambition since a small girl. Oh, Clyde, it was worth coming to Knysna just for this. Dad would never take me — he seemed to dislike the sea. But I just love it." Her blue eyes shone like sapphires.

He fought back a strong impulse to gather her in his arms. But that, he decided, would be taking advantage of the situation. Some other time perhaps. It was sufficient reward to see the pleasure in her eyes, the smile of anticipation on her sweet lips.

He himself was not too eager to take the boat out to sea. He did not consider himself an experienced enough sailor. A leisurely cruise on the lagoon would have satisfied him. But for Penny's sake, to give her the excitement she wanted, he would willingly take "Sally" out into the middle of the ocean.

As the boat sprang into life, Penny gave a little cry of ecstasy.

143

Expertly Clyde steered "Sally" down the lagoon, guiding her through the Heads and out into the ocean. A gentle breeze, coming from the south, ruffled her hair and tugged at her cardigan.

But she didn't care. Gleefully she laughed through the windshield at her companion.

"This is the life for me," she cried exultantly.

Clyde took his gaze off the helm to glance at her with affection. It was good to see the roses back on her cheeks, the laughter in her eyes. She appeared completely to have forgotten Michael Ashmore.

It was too soon, Clyde reckoned, to speak to her of his own love. Perhaps at Christmas . . . . They would both be returning home on the twenty-third. Perhaps he could persuade Penny to join his family at Constantia.

"Are you thinking of going anywhere for Christmas?" he asked, as she appeared at his side.

"Haven't given it a thought yet." Her gaze was on the small white crested waves.

"What about coming to Constantia? I know Leonora would welcome you."

"I'd love to come. If you think it's no trouble — "

"Not at all. Next time I phone home, I'll suggest it to Leonora," Clyde promised, his heartbeats quickening at the idea of having Penny with him.

"When are you due back at the hospital, Clyde?" She was still standing at his side.

"At the beginning of January. That reminds me — I don't think I've mentioned it yet — but I've been successful in my application as Junior Medical Registrar."

She clapped her hands in pleasure. "Good! You deserve it, Clyde." Then she exclaimed, "Oh, goodness!" as a huge spray washed swiftly over the deck. Another followed in its wake.

"High time we went back." His face grew suddenly grave. They had cruised further than he had intended.

"Must we?"

He nodded. "Sorry to disappoint you, Penny. But we must. See those white puffs of cloud? A southeaster is springing up." Frowning, he began to steer the boat around.

"It's all so exciting. I'm enjoying this tremendously, Clyde."

He didn't speak. The white crested waves were growing bigger and more powerful. He opened up the throttle.

"Hold on!" he called to Penny above the roar of the engine.

144

She drew a scarf around her throat and buttoned her cardigan. A boisterous wind buffeted the windshield.

"You'd better sit down, Penny. You'll lose your balance."

She laughed gaily. "This is fun!"

But the smile soon receded from her face as the great rolling swell came right at them. The sun was hiding its face behind thick white clouds.

Anxious trepidations clutched at her heart.

"You all right, Penny?" There was concern on his face.

An impulse to lay her cheek against his sturdy shoulders was strong and sudden.

"I'm fine," she responded, her teeth beginning to chatter.

"I think," he said resolutely, "you had better sit down."

"I'd rather stand here next to you." Her eyes were oddly wistful. "The truth is I'm a little afraid," she confessed with a grimace.

Suddenly there was a lull between the gusts of wind. Clyde put a comforting arm round her slim shoulders.

"That better?" He spoke soothingly.

He is a dear, she mused, feeling a strange stirring within her. *I love Clyde!* The revelation thrilled her. In spite of the cold, a warm glow surged through her.

So much of her heartache, she reflected, could have been avoided had she fallen in love with Clyde in the first place, instead of Michael. But now she knew that she had never really loved Dr. Ashmore. She loved Clyde, not with the illogical passion she had cherished for the medical superintendent. She loved Clyde for what he was — she loved him for himself.

She smiled up at him. He caught the look of wonder in her eyes.

"Oh, Clyde," she breathed against his shoulders. Tears of joy welled up in her eyes.

The wind roared loudly in their ears. Swiftly Clyde withdrew his arm to clutch the helm firmly with both hands. Next instant a heavy swell washed over the deck.

She stood irresolute, then sat down. Her fears had returned. She clasped her hands tightly together to stop their trembling.

She did not want to die just yet. Now that she had found life, the only life that mattered, and love, she wanted to go on living. Life with the Lord was sweet and wonderful. Would it be presumptuous for her to pray that God would spare their lives?

She was still a young convert. As yet, she did not know much about communion with her Lord. She could only hope that He would hear her, that He would "lend a listening ear." Reverently she bowed her head.

At first she found it difficult to pray. Yesterday the Lord had seemed so close; she had been sweetly conscious of His presence. Now He seemed far away.

Then the words she had read from the Scriptures that morning in Hebrews 13:5 came back to her with calm reassurance. "He hath said, I will never leave thee, nor forsake thee."

Dare she claim that promise? Penny wondered a little doubtfully. The Lord had declared He would never leave her — He "Who His own self bare our sins in His own body on the tree." She remembered yesterday seeing those precious words when she had read through I Peter 2.

Yes, the Lord had redeemed her. She now belonged to Him. She was His child. By faith she had accepted His salvation; by faith she must believe the written word, the Bible.

She would not doubt any more. Too long she had deliberately dwelt in darkness. Consequently she had suffered, too. She had trusted man instead of God. She had placed Dr. Ashmore on a pedestal and had worshiped him as a god.

Now all that was finished. It was in the past — the past which God in His love had blotted out. The future was hers to enjoy.

But as Penny glanced out to sea, her heart quailed. The great rolling swell was coming straight at them, drenching the deck and windshield.

"Lord, don't let me be afraid; help me to trust You." She buried her head in her hands, shutting out the cruel, cold sea.

For what seemed like an interminable time, she sat with bowed head. Then gradually His peace, His calmness stole over her. The Lord was with her. Conscious of His presence, she was afraid no longer.

The eyes she raised were as azure and tranquil as a still summer's day.

Then she became aware of Clyde battling against the elements. How strong, how fearless he looked! Though his face was set in determined lines, she perceived that he was perfectly at peace. That inward strength of his, the Lord's strength, had come to his aid when it was most needed.

A song of praise filled her heart as Clyde steered "Sally" through the Heads and into the shelter of the lagoon.

CHAPTER TWENTY-THREE

By four o'clock in the afternoon the southeaster subsided as swiftly as it had sprung up.

Penny and Clyde were sipping tea on the restaurant veranda. All signs of a storm had disappeared. Waves lapped smoothly over the rocks; the crystal surface of the lagoon lay still in the slanting rays of the sun.

Clyde's eyes were tender as he gazed across at Penny. After a warm bath, she had changed into an attractive summer frock. She was smiling shyly, a look of wonder still in her eyes.

Out there in the storm she had found love. She loved the young doctor, not in the way she had loved Michael Ashmore. Her passion for Michael had been stormy and uncontrolled, like the wild, raging sea. Her love for Clyde was infinitely more precious and enduring, tender and sweet and soothing to her nerves. Clyde was far more necessary to her than Dr. Ashmore had ever been or could ever become.

"Feeling all right?" Clyde's voice broke gently into her meditations.

Contentedly she nodded. "I'm fine. Thanks to you. You were splendid, Clyde." He observed the admiration in her eyes.

He sat silent a moment. Then earnestly he exclaimed: "Please don't make me out to be a hero. I wouldn't like that at all. The same as you, I was afraid. Not for myself, but for you. If anything had happened to you — The Lord heard my prayer and He gave me courage and strength to carry on. I blame myself for taking 'Sally' out so far."

"No, Clyde. I'm to blame. I was the one who persuaded you to take the boat out to sea." She halted suddenly. "I also prayed, Clyde. At first I found it difficult — I didn't have much faith.

147

I was terrified — truly I was. But the Lord had mercy on me — He heard my cry and now we're both safe and none the worse for our ordeal."

All the same, Penny mused, *I'm glad it happened. Out there in the stormy sea, I found love. Oh, Clyde, I love you so much!*

But, she reminded herself, *he doesn't love me. There's that girl he's keen on — the one who loves someone else.*

Maybe by now he had given up all thoughts of marrying her. In many ways Clyde was a realist; he would not continue to dream of someone who was unattainable. He was far too sensible and practical for that. Not like herself, Penny smiled wryly.

"Clyde," she began a little diffidently, "have you heard from your girl friend?"

He threw Penny a baffled glance.

"You know, the one who is in love with someone else."

He smiled enigmatically. "Yes, I have heard from her. Just when I was beginning to give up all hope of hearing from her, I came across her suddenly. For months I have been praying for her. She now belongs to the Lord — she has trusted Him for salvation."

"That — that's marvelous news, Clyde." Penny's faltering voice was a mere whisper. "Do — do you still love her?"

"I do." He nodded emphatically. "More than ever."

"Oh." Penny's heart gave a lurch of despair. "But what of the man she's keen on? Doesn't she still care for him?"

"Apparently not. At least, that's what she has told me. She doesn't feel the same for him any more."

"There's a chance then — " Penny took a deep breath, "that she may turn to you."

"I hope so. I sincerely hope so. I have been praying along those lines."

He rose abruptly. "Let's go for a stroll, Penny. I'd like to speak to you."

Feeling slightly dazed, she accompanied him up the little path along the edge of the cliff.

Under a canopy of leafy branches he stopped. Turning to face her, he placed both his hands on her shoulders and peered deep into her blue eyes — eyes which were clouded with confusion.

"Penny," he murmured huskily, "can't you tell?"

"What, Clyde?" Her breath came unevenly. Then, as she forced herself to meet his gaze, a song of rapture filled her heart.

148

Clyde loved her!

"It's been you all the time, Penny. There's been no one else but you. I love you, my dearest girl."

"Oh, Clyde, I can scarcely believe it!" Exquisite joy made her senses real. "It's all so incredible, so glorious. I love you, too, my darling."

He gathered her into his strong arms and, holding her close, he kissed the sweet lips raised so invitingly to his.

A few days later Penny received a letter from Ruth.

"She would like me to be bridesmaid." Penny showed Clyde the letter. "Your sister has consented to be matron of honor."

"Hope you will agree."

Penny nodded enthusiastically. "I will! It will be an honor. I can never thank Ruth enough for taking Michael away from me. Only she didn't do anything of the sort. Michael belonged to me only in my dreams."

"And I?" Clyde's eyes were filled with love.

"You belong here in my heart. Oh, won't they be surprised and pleased to know how things are between us! Michael may even ask you to be best man."

"The chief is sure to ask one of his colleagues. I'm not important enough to fill such a role. I'm only a humble intern — "

"Not any more. Remember you'll be going back to Oakhurst Hospital as medical registrar. And I will return as Dr. Ashmore's secretary until I marry you. Ruth says here that the present secretary will be leaving at the end of the year. It was not a permanent appointment. They were hoping I would return."

"Will that be wise?" She caught the anxious note in Clyde's voice.

Penny darted a mischievous glance at him. "Why not? I'm free of a dream. So there's no need for you to worry."

He came across to where she stood. The sunlight caressed her chestnut hair. Her eyes shone with tenderness. She was altogether adorable.

"I love you, Penny. I love and trust you. Promise me you'll always love me." His arms went around her in a loving embrace.

"I promise," she rejoined solemnly, resting her head on his shoulder.

"To me," she whispered, "you are the most important man in the world. You are more dear and precious than Michael ever was."